Sigismond Lasar

English Anthems

Sigismond Lasar

English Anthems

ISBN/EAN: 9783741191473

Manufactured in Europe, USA, Canada, Australia, Japa

Cover: Foto ©Andreas Hilbeck / pixelio.de

Manufactured and distributed by brebook publishing software
(www.brebook.com)

Sigismond Lasar

English Anthems

TO those who desire, and are willing to labor for, a devouter style of music in the Services of the Church, this Book of Anthems is offered by the compiler.

He believes that to England belongs the honor of producing that music which is most appropriate for ecclesiastical uses—hence, he has prepared a series of "ENGLISH ANTHEMS." From the wealth of existing compositions he has selected only those which in his own experience have proved of great value in the several Churches where he has served as Choir Master.

The success attending the use of these Anthems has not been dependent upon extraordinary skill on the part of the Choirs, which have not in every case been composed of the best material.

The Compiler has arranged the contents of his collection in the order of the Festivals and other Services of the Christian year.

Brief biographical notices of the Composers are appended to the series.

With the sincere hope that it may assist to deepen the love of pure music in American Churches, and thereby to dignify and adorn the public worship of God, this Book of ENGLISH ANTHEMS is presented to the notice of Ministers, Choirs, and Congregations.

English Anthems.

It is high Time to awake out of Sleep.

* Whenever the word "Verse" occurs it is optional to have it sung by one voice or all the voices on the part.

It is high Time to awake out of Sleep.

sleep, for now is our sal - va - tion near-er than when we believ'd, now is our sal - va - tion
sleep, for now is our sal - va - tion near-er than when we be-liev-ed, now is our sal - va - tion
sleep, for now is our sal - va - tion near-er than when we believ'd, now is our sal - va - tion
sleep, for now is our sal - va - tion near-er than when we believ'd, now is our sal - va - tion
VERSE.
near-er than when we be-liev - ed. It is high time to a - wake out of sleep.
near-er than when we be-liev - ed. to a - wake out of sleep.
VERSE.
near-er than when we be-liev - ed. to a - wake out of sleep.
near-er than when we be-liev - ed. It is time to a - wake out of sleep.
p
Ped.
pp VERSE. cres - - - - cen - - - do.
The night is far spent, far. spent, the day is at hand, the day...... is at
The night is far spent, far spent, the day is at hand,.... the day is at
pp VERSE. cres - - - - cen - - - do.
The night is far spent, far... spent, the day is at hand, the day is at
The night is far spent, far... spent, the day is at hand, the day is at
pp Org. ad lib. cres - - - - cen - - - do.

It is high Time to awake out of Sleep.

ROMANS XIII. 12.

MONTEM SMITH.

The Night is far spent.

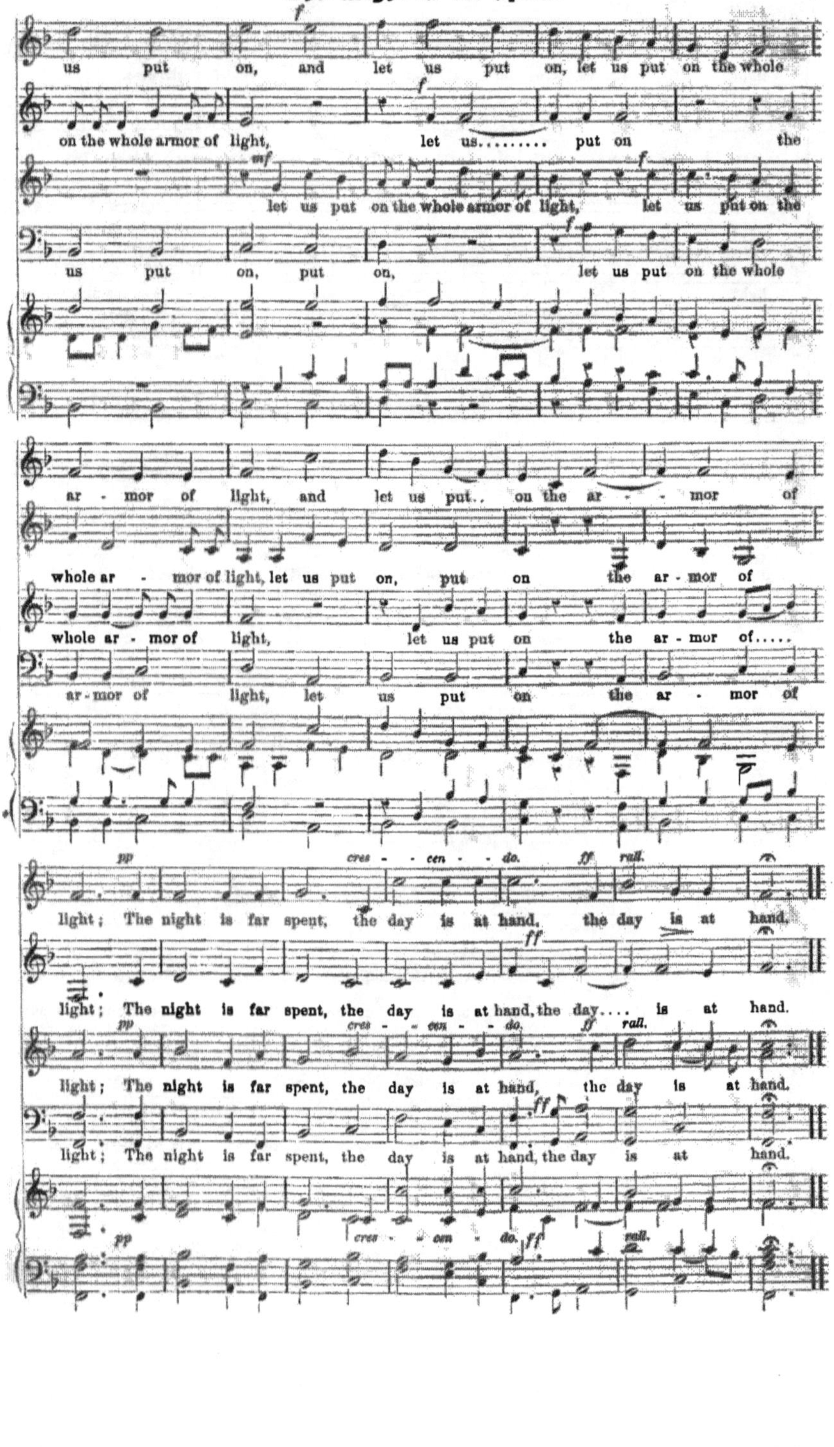
us put on, and let us put on, let us put on the whole
on the whole armor of light, let us......... put on the
let us put on the whole armor of light, let us put on the
us put on, put on, let us put on the whole
ar - mor of light, and let us put.. on the ar - - mor of
whole ar - mor of light, let us put on, put on the ar - mor of
whole ar - mor of light, let us put on the ar - mor of.....
ar - mor of light, let us put on the ar - mor of
pp cres - cen - do. ff rall.
light; The night is far spent, the day is at hand, the day is at hand.
light; The night is far spent, the day is at hand, the day.... is at hand.
light; The night is far spent, the day is at hand, the day is at hand.
light; The night is far spent, the day is at hand, the day is at hand.

Arise, shine, for thy Light is come.

Isaiah LX. 1, 2, 3.

Sir GEORGE JOB ELVEY, Mus. D. (1816 ——).

dark - ness shall cov - er the earth, and gross dark - ness, and gross dark - ness,
dark - ness shall cov - er the earth, and gross dark - ness, and gross dark - ness,
dark - ness shall cov - er the earth, and gross dark - ness, and gross dark - ness,
dark - ness shall cov - er the earth, and gross dark - ness, and gross dark - ness,
gross dark - ness the peo - ple. gross dark - ness the
gross dark - ness the peo - ple, gross dark - ness the
gross dark - ness the peo - ple, gross dark - ness the
gross dark - ness the peo - ple, gross dark - ness the
peo - ple; but the Lord shall a - rise, the Lord shall a - rise, the
peo - ple; but the Lord shall a - rise, the Lord shall a - rise, the
peo - ple; but the Lord shall a - rise, the Lord shall a - rise, the
peo - ple; but the Lord shall a - rise, the Lord shall a - rise, the

Lord shall a - rise up - on thee, and His glo - ry shall be seen, His glo-
Lord shall a - rise up - on...... thee, and His glo - ry shall be seen, His
Lord shall a - rise up - on........ thee, and His glo - ry shall be seen, His
Lord shall a - rise up - on thee, and His glo - ry shall be seen, His
- - ry shall be seen, His glo - ry shall be seen up - on..... thee, And the
glo - ry shall be seen, His glo - ry shall........ be seen up - on thee, And the
glo - ry shall be seen, shall........ be.... seen up - on.... thee, And the
glo - ry shall be seen, His glo - ry shall be seen up - on thee, And the
Gen - tiles shall come, shall come to thy light, and kings..... to the bright ....
Gen - tiles shall come, shall come to thy light, and kings........... to the
Gen - tiles shall come, shall come to thy light, and kings .... to the
Gen - tiles shall come, shall come to thy light, and kings........... to the

- - ness...... of thy ris - ing, and kings........ to the bright - ness, the
bright - ness of thy ris - ing, and kings to the bright - ness,
bright - ness..... of thy ris - ing, kings.... to the bright - ness,
bright - ness of thy ris - ing, and kings to the bright - ness,
bright - - ness.... of thy ris - ing. A - rise, a - rise,
the bright - ness of thy ris - ing. A - rise, a - - rise,
the bright - ness...... of thy ris - ing., A - rise, a - rise, shine,...
the bright - ness of thy ris - ing. A - rise, a - rise,
shine, for thy light is come, shine, for thy light is come, thy light is come.
shine, for thy light is come, shine, for thy light is come, thy light..... is come.
..... for thy light is come, shine,.... for thy light is come, thy light.... is come.
shine, for thy light is come, shine, for thy light is come, thy light is come.

The Grace of God that bringeth Salvation.

Titus II. 11; Psalm xcviii. 3; St. John I. 4.

JOSEPH BARNBY (1838——).

world.......... have seen, have seen the sal - va - tion of our God,.....
world. have seen, have seen the sal - va - tion of our God, our
world.......... have seen, have seen the sal - va - tion of our God, our
world.......... have seen, have seen the sal - va - tion of our God,. ...
all the ends of the world have seen the sal - va - tion of our God.
God, all the ends of the world have seen the sal - va - tion of our God.
God, all the ends of the world have seen the sal - va - tion of our God.
all the ends of the world have seen the sal - va - tion of our God.
Larghetto sostenuto. ♩ = 52.
SOLO—SOPRANO.
Bless-ed, bless-ed be He.... that com-eth,

Blessed, bless-ed be He that com-eth in... the name of........ the Lord, in... the name
of the Lord, Blessed, blessed be He, be He... that cometh in the
cres - - - cen - - do. f dim. p
name of the Lord, Blessed be He, He.. that com-eth.. in the name of the Lord, Blessed,
blessed be He.. that cometh, Blessed, bless-ed be He that cometh in... the name of....... the
dim. e rall.
Lord, that cometh in... the name of the Lord, In the name of the Lord.
dim. e rall.
cres.
pp
Ped.

CHORUS. Allegro moderato. ♩ = 108

Ho-san-na, Ho-san-na in the high - est, Ho-san-na in the high-

Ho-san-na, Ho-san - na in the high-est, Ho-san-na in the high-

Ho-san-na, Ho-san - na in the high - est, Ho-san-na in the high-

Ho-san-na, Ho-san - na in the high - est, Ho-san-na in the high -

f

f

est, Ho-san-na, Ho-san-na in the high - - - est, Ho-san-na, Ho-san-na in the

est, Ho-san-na, Ho-san - na in the high - - est, Ho-san - - na, Ho-

est, Ho-san-na, Ho-san - na in the high - - - est, Ho-san - - - na, Ho-

est, Ho-sa-na, Ho-san - na in the high - - est, in the high - - - - -

mf

high - est. In Him was Life, and the Life was the Light of men ! the

san - - na. In Him was Life, In Him was Life, and

mf

san - - na. In Him was Life,......... In Him was Life,.............. and...

- - - est. In Him was Life, and the Life was the Light of men ! the

mf

The Grace of God that bringeth Salvation.

est, Ho-san-na in the high-est, Ho-san-na, Ho-san-na in the high-est, Ho-
est, Ho-san-na in the high-est, Ho-san-na, Ho-san-na in the high-est, Ho-
est, Ho-san-na in the high-est, Ho-san-na, Ho-san-na in the high-est, Ho-
est, Ho-san-na in the high-est, Ho-san-na, Ho-san-na in the high-est, in the
san-na in the high-est, Ho-san-na in the high-est, Ho-san na,
san-na in the high-est, Ho-san-na in the high-est, Ho-san na,
san-na in the high-est, Ho-san-na in the high-est, Ho-san na,
high na,
Ped.
na, Ho-san-na, Ho-san-na, Ho-san na,
na, Ho-san-na, Ho-san-na, Ho-san na,
na, Ho-san-na, Ho-san-na, Ho-san na,
est, Ho-san-na, Ho-san-na, Ho-san na,

Behold, I bring you good Tidings.

St. Luke ii, 10, 11.

Sir JOHN GOSS, Mus. D. (1800—1880).

Allegro. ♩ = 104.

be to all people, all peo - - ple.
be to all people, all peo - - ple.
be to all people, all peo - ple.
be to all people, all peo - - ple.
For un - to you is born this day,...... in the cit - y of Da-vid, a
For un - to you is born this day,...... in the cit - y of Da-vid, a
8ves.
For un - to you is born this day,........ in the
For un - to you is born this day, in the cit - y, the
Sav - iour, Which is Christ the Lord; For un - to you is born this day,........ in the
Sav - iour, Which is Christ the Lord; For un - to you is born this day, in the cit - y, the
8ves..........

cit-y of Da-vid, a Sav - iour, a Sav - iour, a Saviour, Which is Christ, a
cit-y of Da-vid, a Sav - iour, a Sav - iour, a Saviour, Which is Christ, a
cit-y of Da-vid, a Sav - iour, a Sav - iour, a Saviour, Which is Christ, a
cit-y of Da-vid, a Sav - iour, a Sav - iour, a Saviour, Which is Christ, a
Sav - iour, Which is Christ,.... Which is Christ the Lord.
Sav - iour, Which is Christ the Lord, is Christ.... the Lord.
Sav - iour, Which is Christ,.... Which is Christ the Lord.
Sav - iour, Which is Christ, is Christ the Lord.
Be - hold! I bring you good ti-dings, I bring you good tidings of great joy, which shall
Be - hold! I bring you good ti-dings, I bring you good tidings of great joy, which shall
Be - hold! I bring you good ti-dings, I bring you good tidings of great joy, which shall
Be - hold! I bring you good ti-dings, I bring you good tidings of great joy, which shall

be to all people. For un - to you is born this day, this day, in the cit - y of Da - vid, For
be to all people. For un - to you is born this day, in the cit - y, the cit - y of Da - vid, For
be . to all people. For un - to you is born this day, in the cit - y, the cit - y of Da - vid, For
be to all people. For un - to you is born this day, For
. un - to you is born this day, ... in the cit - y of Da - vid, a Sav - iour, Which is
un - to you is born this day, in the cit - y, the cit - y of Da - vid, a Sav - iour, Which is
un - to you is born this day, ... in the cit - y of Da - vid, a Sav - iour, Which is
un - to you is born this day, in the cit - y, the cit - y of Da - vid, a Sav - iour, Which is
Christ, .. a Sav - iour, Which is Christ .. the ..... Lord....
Christ, .. a Sav - iour, Which is Christ .. the ... Lord...
Christ, a Sav - iour, Which is Christ. the ..... Lord...
Christ, a Sav - iour, Which is Christ. the ..... Lord....
Più lento.

Behold, I bring you glad Tidings.

CHARLES W. SMITH.

CHORUS. p
For un-to you is.. born this day a... Sav-iour, Which is
For un-to you is born this day a Sav-iour, Which is
For un-to you is... born this day a... Sav-iour, Which is..
For un-to you is born this day a Sav-iour, Which is
ff p
Christ the Lord; For un-to you is... born this day a... Sav-iour,
Christ the Lord; For un-to you is born this day a Sav-iour,
Christ the Lord; For un-to you is born this day a Sav-iour,
Christ the Lord; For un-to you is born this day a Sav-iour,
ff p
ff
Which is Christ the Lord. Glo-ry, glo-ry, glo-ry to God,
Which is.. Christ the Lord. Glo-ry, glo-ry, glo-ry to God,
Which is Christ the Lord. Glo-ry, glo-ry, glo-ry to God,
Which is Christ the Lord. Glo-ry be to God in the high- -est,
ff
Ped.

Behold, I bring you glad Tidings.

ff piu mosso.
ff
Al - le - lu - ia, Al - le - lu - ia, A - men. Al - le - lu - ia, Al - le - lu - ia,
Al - le - lu - ia, Al - le - lu - ia, A - men. Al - le - lu - ia, Al - le - lu - ia,
ff
Al - le - lu - ia, Al - le - lu - ia, A - men. Al - le - lu - ia, Al - le - lu - ia,
Al - le - lu - ia, Al - le - lu - ia, A - men. Al - le - lu - ia, Al - le - lu - ia,
ff piu mosso.
ff
Ped.
A - men. For un - to you is born this day a Saviour, Which is Christ the
A - men. For un - to you is born this day a Saviour, Which is Christ the
A - men. For un - to you is born this day a Saviour, Which is Christ the
A - men. For un - to you is born this day a Saviour, Which is Christ the
f
ff molto rall.
Lord, Which is Christ the Lord, Al - le - lu - ia, Al - le - lu - ia, A - - men.
Lord, Which is Christ the Lord, Al - le - lu - ia, Al - le - lu - ia, A - - men.
ff
Lord, Which is Christ the Lord, Al - le - lu - ia, Al - le - lu - ia, A - - men.
Lord, Which is Christ the Lord, Al - le - lu - ia, Al - le - lu - ia, A - - men.
Lord, Which is Christ the Lord, Al - le - lu - ia, Al - le - lu - ia, A - - men.
molto rall.
ff
Ped.

Let us now go even unto Bethlehem.

St. Luke ii. 15, 16, 11.

EDWARD JOHN HOPKINS, Mus. D. (1818 ——).

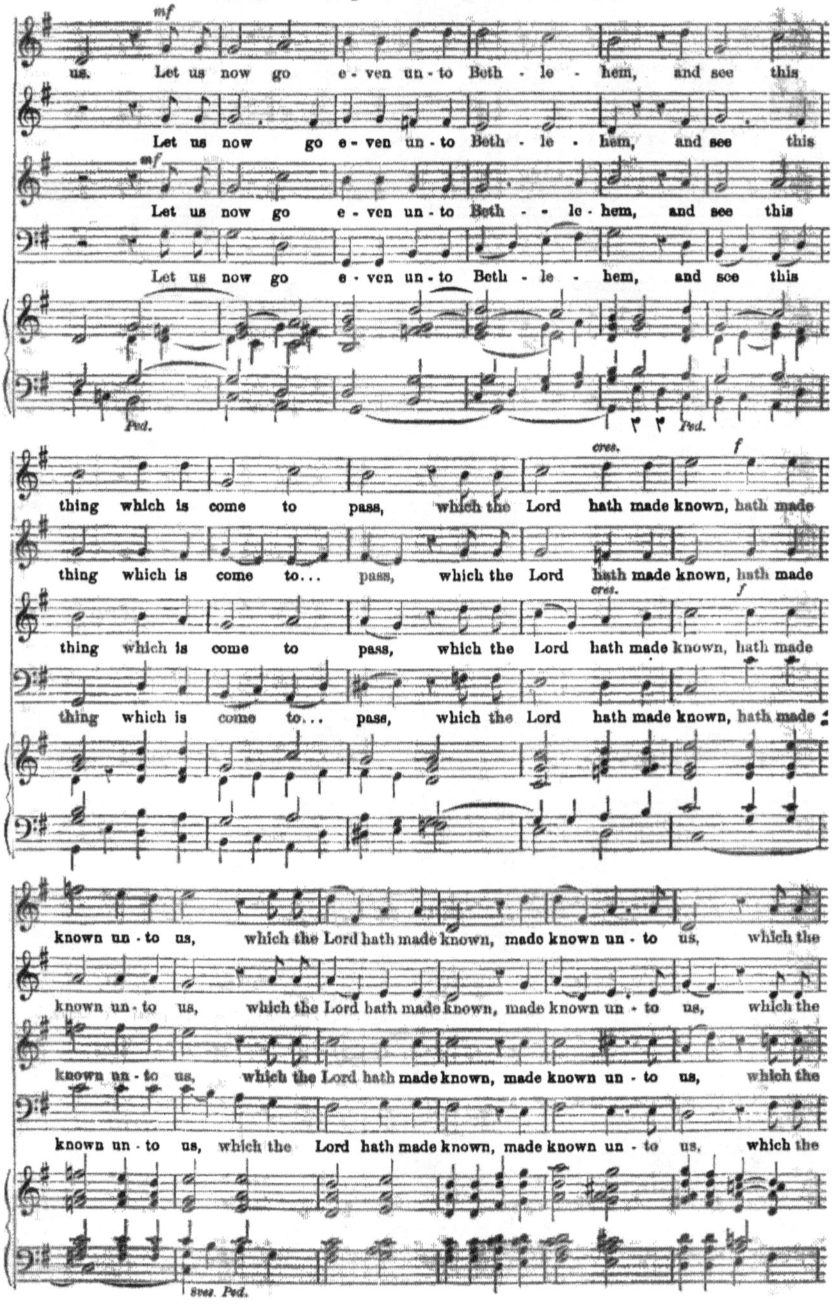
mf
us. Let us now go e - ven un - to Beth - le - hem, and see this
Let us now go e - ven un - to Beth - le - hem, and see this
mf
Let us now go e - ven un - to Beth - - le - hem, and see this
Let us now go e - ven un - to Beth - le - hem, and see this
Ped.
Ped.
cres. f
thing which is come to pass, which the Lord hath made known, hath made
thing which is come to... pass, which the Lord hath made known, hath made
cres. f
thing which is come to pass, which the Lord hath made known, hath made
thing which is come to... pass, which the Lord hath made known, hath made
known un - to us, which the Lord hath made known, made known un - to us, which the
known un - to us, which the Lord hath made known, made known un - to us, which the
known un - to us, which the Lord hath made known, made known un - to us, which the
known un - to us, which the Lord hath made known, made known un - to us, which the
8ves. Ped.

Let us now go even unto Bethlehem.

* Pastoral Symphony from HANDEL's " Messiah."

Let us now go even unto Bethlehem.

In the Beginning was the Word.

St. John i. 1—14; St. Mark xi. 9, 10.

EDWARD HENRY THORNE (1834 ——).

Maestoso. ♩ = 72.

CHORUS.

In the Beginning was the Word.

In the Beginning was the Word.

In the Beginning was the Word.

san - na! Ho - san - na!
Bless-ed is He That
san - na! Ho - san - na!
san - na! Ho - san - na!
Bless-ed is He That com
san - na! Ho - san - na!
Bless-ed is He That com - eth in the Name of the
Largo. ♩ = 48.
ff
com-eth in the Name of the Lord.
Ho-
Bless-ed is He That com - eth.
Ho-
eth in the Name of the Lord.
Ho - san - na!
Ho
Lord, in the Name of the Lord.
Ho - san - na! .... Ho - san - na...
ff
a tempo.
san - na .... in the high - est.
san - na .... in the high - est.
san - na .... in the high - est.
Ho - san - na .... in the high - est.
fff
a tempo.

Sing and Rejoice.

JOSEPH BARNBY (1838 ——).

ZECHARIAH II. 10—13.

Allegro vivace. ♩ = 60.

sing and re - joice,
sing and re - joice,
sing and re - joice, for lo, lo, come, saith the Lord,
sing and re - joice, for lo, lo, I come, saith the Lord,
lo, lo, I come, saith the Lord, will
and I will dwell in the midst of thee,
and I will dwell in the midst of thee,
dwell in the midst of thee, saith the Lord........ thy God,
saith the Lord........ thy God,
saith the Lord, saith the Lord........ thy God, lo, I
dwell in the midst of thee, saith the Lord thy God, lo, I

saith the Lord. thy God.
the Lord thy God.
come, and I will dwell in the midst of thee, saith the Lord...... thy God.
come, and I will dwell in the midst of thee, the Lord thy God.
rit. a tempo.
Sing and re-joice,.... O daugh-ter of Si-on, sing,
Sing and re-joice,.... O daugh-ter of Si-on, sing,
rit. a tempo.
Sing and re-joice,.... O daugh-ter of Si-on, sing,
a tempo.
Sing and re-joice,.... O daugh-ter of Si-on, sing,
rit.
Ped.
sing, O sing and re-joice, sing and re-joice,.... O daugh-ter of
sing, O sing and re-joice, sing and re-joice, O daugh-ter of
sing, O sing and re-joice, sing, and re-joice,.... O daugh-ter of
sing, O sing and re-joice, sing and re-joice,.... O daugh-ter of

Si - on, sing, sing, O sing and re - joice. Be si - lent,
Si - on, sing, sing, O sing and re - joice. Be si - lent,
Si - on, O sing, sing, O sing and re - joice. Be si - lent,
Si - on, sing, sing, O sing and re - joice. Be si - lent,
si - lent, O all flesh, be-fore the Lord, be-fore the Lord, for
si - lent, O all flesh, be-fore the Lord, be-fore the Lord, for He is
si - lent, O all flesh, be-fore the Lord, be-fore the Lord, for He is
si - lent, O all flesh, be-fore the Lord, be-fore the Lord, for
He is rais - ed up, is rais - ed up out of His ho - ly ha - bi-
rais - ed up, for He is rais - ed up out of His ho - ly ha - bi-
rais - ed up, for He is rais - ed up out of His ho - ly ha - bi.
He is rais - ed up out of His ho - ly ha - bi-

Sing and Rejoice.

tion. Sing and re-joice...... O daugh-ter of Si-on, sing,
-tion. Sing and re-joice,...... O daugh-ter of Si-on, sing,
ta-tion. Sing and re-joice,...... O daugh-ter of Si-on, sing,
tion. Sing and re-joice,...... O daugh-ter of Si-on, sing,
sing, O sing and re-joice, sing and re-joice,...... O daugh-ter of
sing, O sing and re-joice, sing and re-joice,...... O daugh-ter of
sing, O sing and re-joice, sing and re-joice,...... O daugh-ter of
sing, O sing and re-joice, sing and re-joice,...... O daugh-ter of
Si-on, sing, sing, O sing and re-joice,
Si-on, sing and re-joice, O sing and re-joice,
Si-on, sing and re-joice, O sing and re-joice, for lo, lo, I
Si-on, sing, sing, O sing and re-joice, for lo, lo, I

Sing and Rejoice.

Beth - le - hem; Come and be - hold Him, Born the King of An - gels; O come let us a-
Beth - le - hem; Come and be - hold Him, Born the King of An - gels; O come let us a-
Beth - le - hem; Come and be - hold Him, Born the King of An - gels; O come let us a-
Beth - le - hem; Come and be - hold Him, Born the King of An - gels; O come let us a-
dore, Him, O come let us a - dore Him, O come let us a - dore Him, Christ the
dore Him, O come let us a - dore Him, O come let us a - dore Him, Christ the
dore Him, O come let us a - dore Him, O come let us a - dore Him, Christ the
dore Him, O come let us a - dore Him, O come let us a - dore Him, Christ the
Lord, A men.
Lord, A men.
Lord, A men.
Lord, A men.
Ped.

Sing, O Heavens.

Isaiah xlix. 13; St. Luke ii. 11; St. Matthew xxi. 9, etc.

BERTHOLD TOURS (1838 ——).

Allegro ma non troppo.
♩. = 104.

sing-ing, and break forth in-to sing-ing, O mountains, O mountains, O mount-
sing-ing, and break forth in-to sing-ing, O mountains, O mountains, O mount-
sing-ing, and break forth in-to sing-ing, O mountains, O mountains, O mount-
sing-ing, and break forth in-to sing-ing, O mountains, O mountains, O mount-
mf f
ains. Sing, O heav-ens, sing, O heav-ens, and be joy-ful, O earth, O
ains. Sing, O heav-ens, sing, O heav-ens, and be joy-ful, O earth, O
ains. Sing, O heav-ens, and be joy-ful, O earth, sing, O
ains. and be joy-ful, O earth, O
mf f
earth, O earth, and be joy-ful, O earth, sing, O
earth, O earth, and be joy-ful, O earth, sing, O
heav-ens, and be joy-ful, and be joy-ful, O earth, sing, O
earth, O earth, and be joy-ful, O earth, sing, O
ff

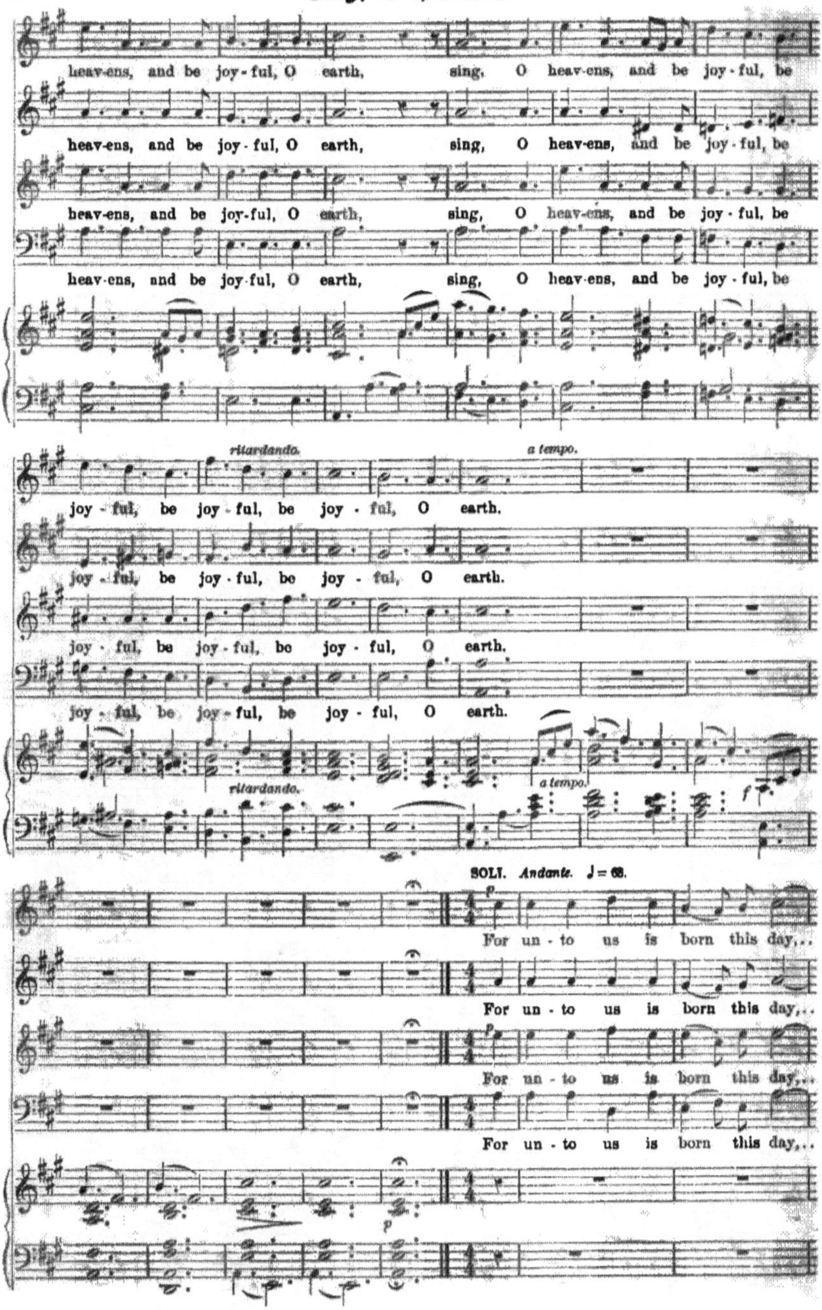
heav-ens, and be joy-ful, O earth, sing, O heav-ens, and be joy-ful, be
heav-ens, and be joy-ful, O earth, sing, O heav-ens, and be joy-ful, be
heav-ens, and be joy-ful, O earth, sing, O heav-ens, and be joy-ful, be
heav-ens, and be joy-ful, O earth, sing, O heav-ens, and be joy-ful, be
ritardando.
a tempo.
joy-ful, be joy-ful, be joy-ful, O earth.
joy-ful, be joy-ful, be joy-ful, O earth.
joy-ful, be joy-ful, be joy-ful, O earth.
joy-ful, be joy-ful, be joy-ful, O earth.
ritardando.
a tempo.
SOLI. Andante. ♩= 68.
For un-to us is born this day,..
For un-to us is born this day,..
For un-to us is born this day,..
For un-to us is born this day,..

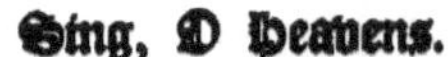

.... in the cit-y of Da-vid, a Sav-iour, Which is Christ the Lord, Which is Christ the
.... in the cit-y of Da-vid, a Sav-iour, Which is Christ the Lord, Which is Christ the
.... in the cit-y of Da-vid, a Sav-iour, Which is Christ the Lord, Which is Christ the
.... in the cit-y of Da-vid, a Sav-iour, Which is Christ the Lord, Which is Christ the
poco rall.
pp
poco rall.
CHORUS. Più animato. ♩ = 80.
Lord. Ho-san-na Ho-san-na, Ho-san-na to the Son of Da-vid.......
Lord. Ho-san-na, Ho-san-na, Ho-san-na to the Son of Da-vid......
Lord. Ho-san-na, Ho-san-na to the Son of Da-vid......
Lord. Ho-san-na, Ho-san-na to the Son of Da-vid......
f Org. ad lib.
senza Ped.
ff Org.
Ped.
mf
p
pp

Sing, O Heavens.

com - eth,   bless - ed is He,........   is He, is.. He, is...
Bless - ed is He That com - eth   in   the   Name,   in   the
Bless - ed is He That com - eth   in   the   Name,   in   the
Bless - ed is He That com - eth   in   the   Name,   in   the
Bless - ed   is   He,   He That
He,................   He That com-eth in the Name of the   Lord...............
Name   of the Lord, in   the   Name   of   the   Lord............
Name   of the Lord, in   the   Name   of   the   Lord............
Name   of the Lord, in   the   Name   of   the   Lord............
com - - - eth   in   the   Name   of   the   Lord............
Poco più Andante.
p   pp
pp
pp

Sing, O Heavens.

men, to God on high be glo - ry, to God on high be glo - ry, to God, to God on
men, to God on high be glo - ry, to God, to God on
men, to God on high be glo - ry, to
men, to God on high, to God on high be glo - ry,
high, to God, to God on high, to God on
high, to God, to God on high, to God on
God, to God on high, on high, to God on
to God on high, to God on high, to God, to God on high, on
high, to God on high, to God on high, to God be glo - ry. O come, all ye faith - ful,
high, to God on high, to God on high, to God be glo - ry. O come, all ye faith - ful,
high, to God on high, to God on high, to God be glo - ry. O come, all ye faith - ful,
high, to God on high, to God on high, to God be glo - ry. O come, all ye faith - ful,
f Tempo 1mo.
f
cres - - - cen - - - do.
ff
cres - - - cen - - - do.
ff
cres.
ff
molto rallentando.
Molto maestoso. ♩ = 58. sempre ff
sempre ff
molto rallentando.
sempre ff

Sing, O Heavens.

St. Luke ii. 10, 11, 14, etc.

JOSEPH BARNBY (1838 —).

Behold, I bring you good Tidings.

ritardando poco a poco.
.... the Lord,........ a Sav - - lour, a
ritardando poco a poco.
cres - - - con - - - - -
ff
Sav - iour, Which is Christ............................... the
ff
do.
Lord.
CHORUS. Allegro. = 112.
f
Glo - ry, glo - ry, glo - ry to God............ in the high - est,
Glo - ry, glo - ry, glo - ry to God............ in the high - est,
f
Glo - ry, glo - ry, glo - ry to God............ in the high - est,
Glo - ry, glo - ry, glo - ry to God............ in the high - est,
f

in the high - est, glo - ry, glo - ry, glo - ry to God,
in the high - est, glo - ry, glo - ry, glo - ry to God, to
in the high - est, glo - ry, glo - ry, glo - ry to God,......
in the high - est, glo - ry, glo - ry, glo - ry to God,......
glo - ry to God in the high - - est, and on earth peace,....
God, to God in the high - - est,...... ... and on
...... to God in the high - - est,......... and on
...... to God............. in the high - est,.... and on
...... and on earth peace,......
earth......... peace,....... peace,....... good
earth......... peace,....... peace,....... good - will to - ward
earth......... peace,....... peace,.......

good-will to-ward men, good-will to-ward
will to-ward men, to-ward men, good-will to-ward men,
men, good-will to-ward men, to -
good will to-ward men, good-
men, good-will, good-will to - ward
to - ward men, good-will, good-will to-ward
ward men, good-will, good-will to-ward
will to-ward men, good-will, good-will to - ward
men, peace and good-will, good-will and peace.
men, peace and good-will, good-will and peace.
men, peace and good-will, good-will and peace.
men, peace and good-will, good-will and peace.

Behold, I bring you good Tidings.

God. in the high - est, in the high - - - est..
God. in the high - est, in the high - - est......
to God in the high - est, in the high - - est......
God............ in the high - est, in the high - - est.....
CHORAL.
O Je - su, born of Vir - gin pure, Im - mor - tal glo - ry be to Thee, Whom
O Je - su, born of Vir - gin pure, Im - mor - tal glo - ry be to Thee, Whom
O Je - su, born of Vir - gin pure, Im - mor - tal glo - ry be to Thee, Whom
O Je - su, born of Vir - gin pure, Im - mor - tal glo - ry be to Thee, Whom
with the Fa - ther we a - dore, And Ho - ly Ghost e - ter - nal - ly. A - - men.
with the Fa - ther we a - dore, And Ho - ly Ghost e - ter - nal - ly. A - - men.
with the Fa - ther we a - dore, And Ho - ly Ghost e - ter - nal - ly. A - - men.
with the Fa - ther we a - dore, And Ho - ly Ghost e - ter - nal - ly. A - - men.

Sing, O Daughter of Zion.

joice with all the heart, O daugh-ter of Je - ru - sa - lem. The King of
joice, re - joice, O daugh-ter of Je - ru - sa - lem. The King of
joice, re - joice, O daugh-ter of Je - ru - sa - lem. The King of
joice, re - joice, O daugh-ter of Je - ru - sa - lem.
Is - ra - el, e - ven the Lord, is in the midst of thee,
Is - ra - el, e - ven the Lord, is in the midst of thee, the King of
Is - ra - el, e - ven the Lord, is in the midst of thee, the King of
The King of
the King of
Is - ra - el, e - ven the Lord, is in the midst of thee,
Is - ra - el, e - ven the Lord, is in the midst of thee, the King
Is - ra - el, e - ven the Lord, is in the midst of thee, the King of

Sing, O Daughter of Zion.

will save,............ He will re - joice o - ver thee with
He.... will save,.... He... will save,........ He will re - joice o - ver thee with
He.... will save,.. He will save........ He will re-
He ... will save,.... He will save,........ He will re-
sempre piano e sostenuto
joy, He will re - joice o - ver thee with joy; He will rest,....
joy, He will re - joice o - ver thee with joy; He will rest, ...
joice o - ver thee with joy,.... He will re - joice o - ver thee with joy;.... He will
joice o - ver thee with joy,.... He will re - joice o - ver thee with joy;.... He will
He will rest,.... He will rest in His love, He will rest,......
He will rest, He will rest in His love, He will rest, ...
rest, He will rest, will rest in His love, He will
rest, He will rest, will rest in His love, He will
Ped.

poco rall.
He will rest,.... He will rest in His love........
He will rest, He will rest in His love........
rest, He will rest, will rest in His love........
rest, He will rest, will rest in His love........
poco rall.
p a tempo. cres.
rall.
.... Sing, O daugh-ter of Zi - on, sing, O daugh-ter of Zi - on, sing, O daugh-ter,
.... Sing, O daugh-ter of Zi - on, sing, O daugh-ter of Zi - on, sing, O daugh-ter,
.... Sing, O daugh-ter of Zi - on, sing, O daugh-ter of Zi - on, sing, O daugh-ter,
.... Sing, O daugh-ter of Zi - on, sing, O daugh-ter of Zi - on, sing, O daugh-ter,
a tempo. cres.
rall.
f a tempo.
sing, O daughter of Zi - on; shout, O Is - ra - el;
sing, O daugh-ter of Zi - on; shout, O Is - ra - el;
sing, O daughter of Zi - on; shout, O Is - ra - el; be glad and re - joice with all the heart, O
sing, O daughter of Zi - on; shout, O Is - ra - el; re - joice, O
a tempo.
f
Ped.

be glad and re - joice with all the heart, O daugh - ter of Je - ru - sa - lem; be
re - joice, O daugh - ter of Je - ru - sa - lem; be
daugh - ter of Je - ru - sa - lem, O daugh - ter of Je - ru - sa - lem; be
daugh - ter, re - joice, O daugh - ter of Je - ru - sa - lem; be
glad and re - joice, re - joice with all the heart, re - joice with all the heart. The
glad and re joice. re - joice with all the heart, re - joice with all the heart. The
glad and re - joice, re - joice with all the heart, re - joice with all the heart. The
glad and re - joice, re - joice, re - joice.............. The
molto lento. molto ritard.
King of Is - ra - el, e - ven the Lord, is in the midst of thee.
King of Is - ra - el, e - ven the Lord, is in the midst of thee.
King of Is - ra - el, e - ven the Lord, is in the midst of thee.
King of Is - ra - el, e - ven the Lord, is in the midst of thee.
rall. ff
molto lento. molto ritard.

In the Beginning was the Word.

St. John i. i, 14; Psalm xlv. 2; St. Luke i. 68.

GEORGE BENJAMIN ALLEN, Mus. B. (1822 ——).

CHORAL RECITATIVE (*accompanied*)—Tenors and Basses.

dwelt a - mong us, the Word..... was made Flesh, the Word was made Flesh, the
dwelt a - mong us, the Word, the Word was made, the Word was made Flesh, the
dwelt a - mong us, the Word, the Word was made, the Word was made Flesh, the
dwelt a - mong us, the Word, the Word was made, the Word was made Flesh, the Word..
Word was made Flesh, and dwelt a - mong us, dwelt a - mong us.
Word was made Flesh, and dwelt a - mong us, dwelt a - mong us.
Word was made Flesh, and dwelt a - mong us, dwelt a - mong us.
..... was made Flesh, and dwelt a - mong us, dwelt a - mong us.
CHORAL RECIT.—TENORS AND BASSES.
And the Word was made Flesh, and dwelt a-mong us, and dwelt a - mong

In the Beginning was the Word.

God hath bless-ed Thee, hath blessed Thee for ev - er, hath blessed Thee for ev - er.
Thou art fair - er than the chil - dren of men, full of grace are Thy lips be - cause
God hath bless-ed Thee, hath blessed Thee for ev - er.
CHORUS. Allegro maestoso.
Bless-ed be the Lord God of Is - ra - el, Bless-ed be the
Bless-ed be the Lord God of Is - ra - el, Bless-ed be the
Bless-ed be the Lord God of Is - ra - el, Bless-ed be the
Bless-ed be the Lord God of Is - ra - el, Bless-ed be the

In the Beginning was the Word.

for He hath vis-it-ed
for He hath vis-it-ed and re-deem-ed His peo-ple.
He hath vis-it-ed and re-deem-ed His peo-ple, and re-deem-ed His peo-ple.
and redeemed His peo-ple, He hath vis-it-ed and re-deem-ed His peo-ple.
and re-deem-ed His peo-ple, and re-deem-ed His peo-ple, He hath vis-it-ed
Bless-ed be God, the Lord God of Is-rael, Bless-ed be the
Bless-ed be the Lord God of Is-rael, Bless-ed be the
Bless-ed be the Lord God of Is-rael, Bless-ed be the
and redeemed His peo-ple,... for He hath vis-it-ed.... and re-deem-ed His peo-ple, His
Lord God of Is-ra-el,.... for He hath vis-it-ed.... and re-deem-ed His peo-ple, His
Lord God of Is-ra-el,.... for He hath vis-it-ed.... and re-deem-ed His peo-ple, His
Lord God of Is-ra-el,.... for He hath vis-it-ed.... and re-deem-ed his peo-ple, His

In the Beginning was the Word.

God of Is - ra - el, for He hath vis - it - ed and re - deem - ed His
God of Is - ra - el, for He hath vis - it - ed and re - deem - ed His
God of Is - ra - el, for He hath vis - it - ed and re - deem - ed His
God of Is - ra - el, for He hath vis - it - ed and re - deem - ed His
fz.
peo - ple, re - deem - ed His peo - ple. Bless - ed be the Lord..........
peo - ple, re - deem - ed His peo - ple. Bless - ed be the Lord..........
peo - ple, re - deem - ed His peo - ple. Bless - ed be the Lord God, the
peo - ple, re - deem - ed His peo - ple. Bless - ed be the Lord..........
Ped.
God of Is - ra - el, A - - men.
God of Is - ra - el, A - - men.
God of Is - ra - el, the God of Is - ra - el. A - - men.
God of Is - ra - el. A - - men.

Blessed be the Lord God of Israel.

St. Luke i. 68—70; ii. 14. Isaiah ix. 6, 7.

SAMUEL SEBASTIAN WESLEY, Mus. D. (1810—1876).

Andante. ♩ = 108.

peo-ple, He hath vis-it-ed and re-deem-ed,.................... and re-
peo-ple, His peo-ple, hath.... He hath vis-it-ed and re-deem-ed, re-
peo-ple, He hath vis-it-ed,.... for He hath
peo-ple, for He hath vis it ed, hath vis-it-ed, and re-
deem-ed, for He hath vis-it-ed and re-deem-ed His peo-ple, He hath
deem-ed, for He hath vis-it-ed and re-deem-ed His peo-ple, He hath
vis-it-ed, for He hath vis-it-ed and re-deem-ed His peo-ple, He hath
deem-ed, for He hath vis-it-ed and re-deem-ed His peo-ple,
vis-it-ed and re-deem-ed His peo-ple,
vis-it-ed and re-deem-ed His peo-ple, And hath rais-ed up a
vis-it-ed and re-deem-ed, And hath rais-ed up a
And hath rais-ed up a horn of sal-va-tion

Blessed be the Lord God of Israel.

God of Is - ra - el, for He hath vis - it - ed and re - deem - ed His peo - ple.
God of Is - ra - el, for He hath vis - it - ed and re - deem - ed His peo - ple.
God of Is - ra - el, for He hath vis - it - ed and re - deem - ed His peo - ple.
God of Is - ra - el, for He hath vis - it - ed and re - deem - ed His peo - ple.
SEMI-CHORUS. Allegro moderato. ♩ = 104.
For un - to us a Child is born, un - to us a Son is giv - en; and the
gov - ernment shall be up - on His shoul - der. For un - to us a Child is born, un - to
ALTO.
us a Son is giv - en; and the gov - ernment shall be up - on His shoul - der.

Blessed be the Lord God of Israel.

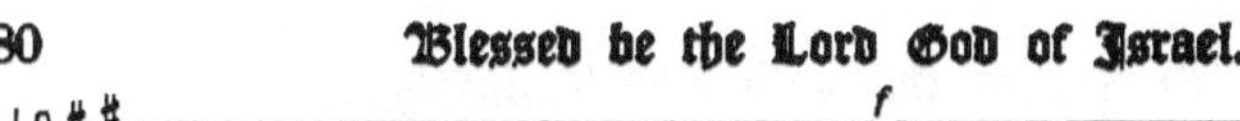

of His gov - ern-ment and peace there shall be no..........
Of the in - crease of His gov - ern-ment and peace there shall
of His gov - ern-ment and peace there shall be no..........
Of the in - crease of His gov - ern-ment and peace there shall
.... end.
be no end.
.... end. The zeal of the Lord of Hosts will per - form......
be no end. The zeal of the Lord of Hosts will per - form......
The zeal of the Lord of Hosts, The zeal of the
The zeal of the Lord of Hosts, The zeal of the
this, The zeal of the Lord of Hosts
this, The zeal of the Lord of Hosts

Blessed be the Lord God of Israel.

Andante. ♩ = 80.
- - ry to God on high. And on earth peace, good-will to-ward men,
- - ry to God.... on high. And on earth peace, good-will to-ward men,
- - ry to God on high. And on earth peace, good-will, good-will to-ward
- - ry to God on high. And on earth peace, good-will to-ward men,
and on earth peace, good-will to-ward men, peace on earth, good - -
peace, peace on earth, good - - will, peace, peace on earth, good-
men, and....... on earth, good - will, good-will, peace, peace on earth, good-
peace, and on earth, and on earth peace,........
will, and on earth peace, good - will to-ward men, and on earth on
will to-ward men, on earth peace, good - will to-ward men, and on earth
will to-ward men, on earth peace, good - will to-ward men, and on earth
peace, and on earth peace, good-will to-ward men, and on earth
dim.
p

Blessed be the Lord God of Israel.

O that I knew where I might find Him.

Job xxiii. 3, 8, 9; St. John xx. 29.

Sir WILLIAM STERNDALE BENNETT, Mus. D., D.C.L. (1816—1875).

O that I knew where I might find Him.

hold Him: He hid-eth Him-self on the right hand, He hid-eth Him-self
hold Him: He hid-eth Him-self, hid-eth Him-self.......... on the
hold Him: He hid-eth Him-self on the right hand,
hold Him: He hid-eth Him-self on the right hand,
on the right hand, hid-eth Him-self,... Him-self on.... the right hand.
...... right hand, He hid-eth him-self on.... the right hand
hid - - eth He hid-eth Him-self on..... the right hand.
hid - - eth, He..... hid-eth Him-self on..... the right hand.
p Arioso moderato. ♩ = 72.
Bless - ed are they, are they that have not seen, that have not
Bless - ed are they, are they that have not seen, that have not
Bless - ed are they, are they that have not seen, that have not seen, not
Bless - - - ed are they that have not seen, not
Ped.
pp
p
cres.

seen, and yet have be - liev - ed. Bless - ed, bless - ed are they that
seen, and yet have be - liev - ed. Bless - ed, bless - ed are they that
seen, and yet have be - liev - ed. Bless - ed are they..........
seen, and yet have be - liev - - - ed. Bless - ed, bless - ed....... are they that
have not seen, that have not seen,....... not seen, and yet have be - liev - ed.
have not seen, not seen, and yet have be - liev - - - ed.
.... that have........ not seen,...... and yet have be - liev - ed.
have not seen, they....... that have not seen, and yet have be - liev - ed.
Bless - ed...... are they.... that have not seen,.... that
Bless - ed...... are they that have not seen,.... are they that have not
Bless - ed...... are they, they that have not seen,.... are they that have not
Bless - ed...... are they, are they,.... are they that have not
senza Ped.

have not, not seen...... that have not seen, and yet have be-
seen, that have not seen, that have not seen, and yet have be-
seen, that have not seen, that have not seen, and yet have be-
seen, that have not seen, that have not seen, and yet have be-
Ped.
liev - ed, Bless - - ed, bless - ed are they that have not seen, that
liev - ed. Bless - ed, bless - ed, bless - - ed are
liev - ed. Bless - - - ed, bless - - ed........ are
liev - - ed. Bless - ed are.... they, are they that have not
have not seen,............. and.... yet have be - liev - ed, that have not
they, and yet, and yet have be - liev - - ed, that have....
they that have not seen, and yet have be - liev - ed, that have not seen,
seen, and yet have be - liev - - ed,..... that have not seen,
senza Ped.

O that I knew where I might find Him.

From the Rising of the Sun.

MALACHI I. II.

THE REV. SIR FREDERICK ARTHUR GORE OUSELEY.
Bart., M.A., Mus. D. (1825 ——).

From the Rising of the Sun.

same My Name shall be great, shall be great a - mong....... the Gen-
same f My Name shall be great a - mong the Gen-
same My Name shall be great, shall be great a - mong the Gen-
same f My Name shall be great a - mong the Gen-
tiles; and in ev - - 'ry place, and in ev - - 'ry place in - cense
tiles; and in ev - - 'ry place, and in ev - - 'ry place in - cense
tiles; and in ev - - 'ry place, and in ev - - 'ry place in - cense
tiles; and in ev - - 'ry place, and in ev - - 'ry place in - cense
shall be of - fer'd up un - to. ...... My Name, thus...... saith the Lord.
shall be of - fer'd up un - to........ My Name, thus............ saith the Lord.
shall be of - fer'd up un - to.... My... Name, thus saith...... the Lord.
shall be of - fer'd up un - to........ My Name, thus saith the Lord.

Lord, for Thy tender Mercies' sake.

RICHARD FARRANT* (circa 1530—1580).

* This Anthem is commonly attributed to FARRANT, but without sufficient grounds. It is attributed by several authorities to JOHN HILTON, Organist of St. Margaret's, Westminster, who died about the middle of the 17th century.

per-fect heart,..... that we may walk with a per-fect heart be-fore Thee now and ev-er-
heart, that we may walk with a per-fect heart be-fore Thee now and ev-er-
heart, that we may walk with a per-fect heart, with a per-fect heart be-fore Thee now and ev-er-
heart, that we may walk with a per-fect heart, with a per fect heart be-fore Thee now and ev-er-
cres.
p
cres.
cres.
more, that we may walk with a per-fect heart,.....
more, that we may walk with a per-fect heart,
more, that we may walk with a per-fect heart, a per-fect heart, that we may
more, that we may walk with a per-fect heart, with a per-fect heart, that we may
f
f
f
f
p rall. e de-cres-cen-do.
..... that we may walk with a per-fect heart be-fore Thee now and ev-er-more.
that we may walk with a per-fect heart be-fore Thee now and ev-er-more.
walk with a per-fect heart, with a per-fect heart be-fore Thee now and ev-er-more.
walk with a per-fect heart, with a per-fect heart be-fore Thee now and ev-er-more.
p rall. e de-cres-cen-do.
p rall. de-cres-cen-do.

Turn Thy Face from my Sins.

* Originally in the Key of E. The Melody of the two divisions of the Anthem, indicated by repeat marks, may first be sung as a Solo.

new a right spir - it with - in...... me. Cast me not a - way........ a-
new a right spir - it with - in.... me. Cast me not a - way....... a-
new a right spir - it with - in.... me, Cast me not a - way...... a-
new a right spir - it with - in me, Cast me not a - way...... a-
way from Thy pres - ence, and take not Thy Ho - ly Spir - it from me, and
way from Thy pres - ence, and take not Thy Ho - ly Spir - it from me, and
way from Thy pres - ence, and take not Thy Ho - ly Spir - it from me, and
way from Thy pres - ence, and take not Thy Ho - ly Spir - it from me,
2d time rallentando.
take not Thy Ho - ly Spir - it from me, Thy Ho - ly Spir - it from me.
take not Thy Ho - ly Spir - it from me, Thy Ho - ly Spir - it from me.
take not Thy Ho - ly Spir - it from me, Thy Ho - ly Spir - it from me.
Thy Ho - ly Spir - it from me.

Enter not into Judgment.

Psalm cxliii. 2. THOMAS ATTWOOD (1767–1838).

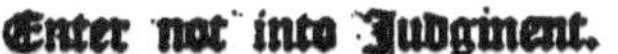

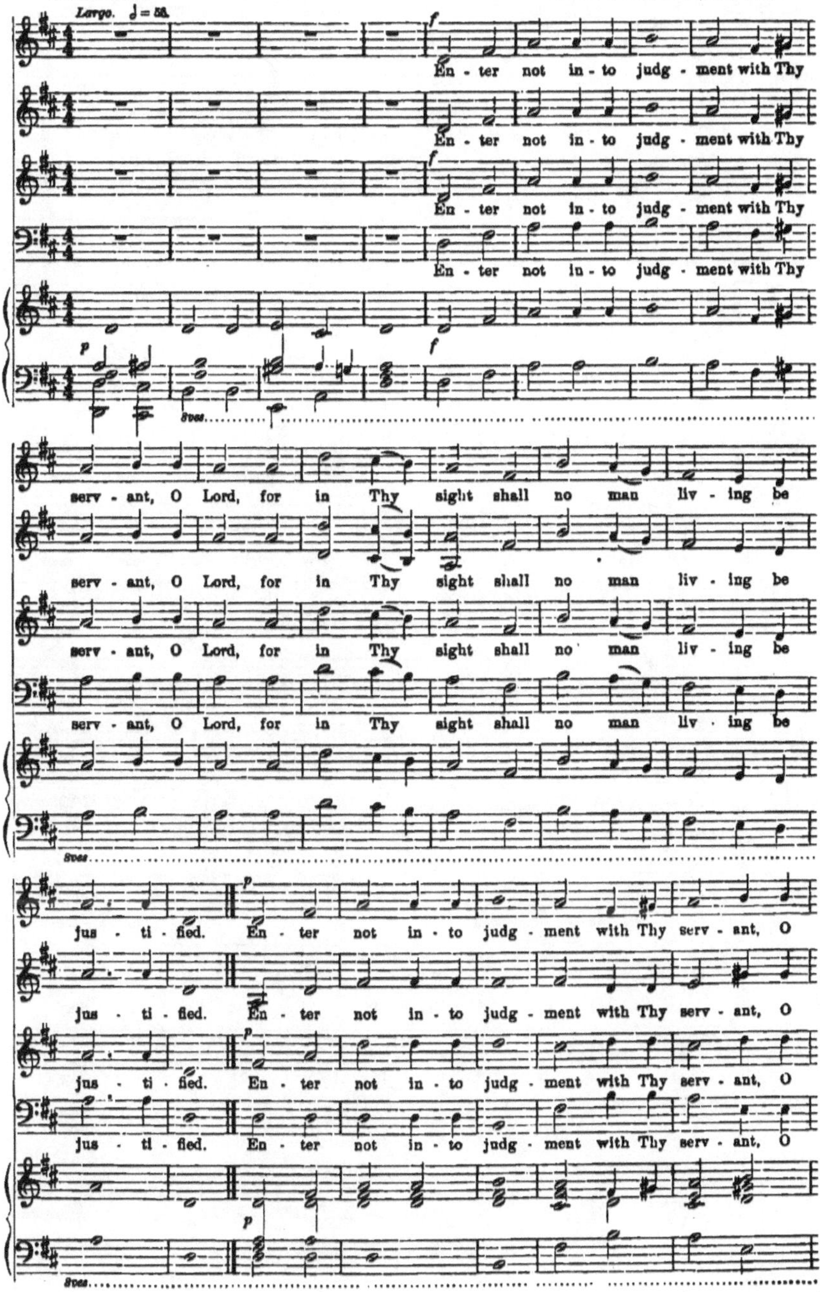

Lord, for in Thy sight shall no man liv-ing be jus-ti-
Lord, for in Thy sight shall no man liv-ing be jus-ti-
Lord, for in Thy sight shall no man liv-ing be jus-ti-
Lord, for in Thy sight shall no man liv-ing be jus-ti-
fied, for in Thy sight shall no man
fied, for in Thy sight, for in Thy sight shall no man
fied, for in Thy sight, for in Thy sight shall no man
fied, for in Thy sight shall no man
liv-ing be jus-ti-fied, for in Thy
liv-ing be jus-ti-fied, for in Thy sight, for in Thy
liv-ing be jus-ti-fied, for in Thy sight, for in Thy
liv-ing be jus-ti-fied, for in Thy sight

sight shall no man liv - ing be jus - ti - fied, shall...... no....
sight shall no man liv - ing be jus - ti - fied, shall...... no....
sight shall no man liv - ing be jus - ti - fied, shall.... be
shall no man liv - ing be jus - ti - fied, shall. no
.... man be jus - ti - fied, no man, no man be jus - ti-
.... man be jus - ti - fied, no man, no man be jus - ti-
man be jus - ti - fied, no man.......... be jus - ti-
man be jus - ti - fied, no man.......... be jus - ti-
1st and 2d.
fied, be jus - ti - fied, be jus - ti - - fied..................
fied, be jus - ti - fied, be jus - ti - fied..................
fied, be jus - ti - fied, be jus - ti - fied..................
fied, be jus - ti - fied, be jus - ti - fied..................

Hear my Prayer, O Lord.

Psalm cxliii. 1. — PETER von WINTER (1754–1825).

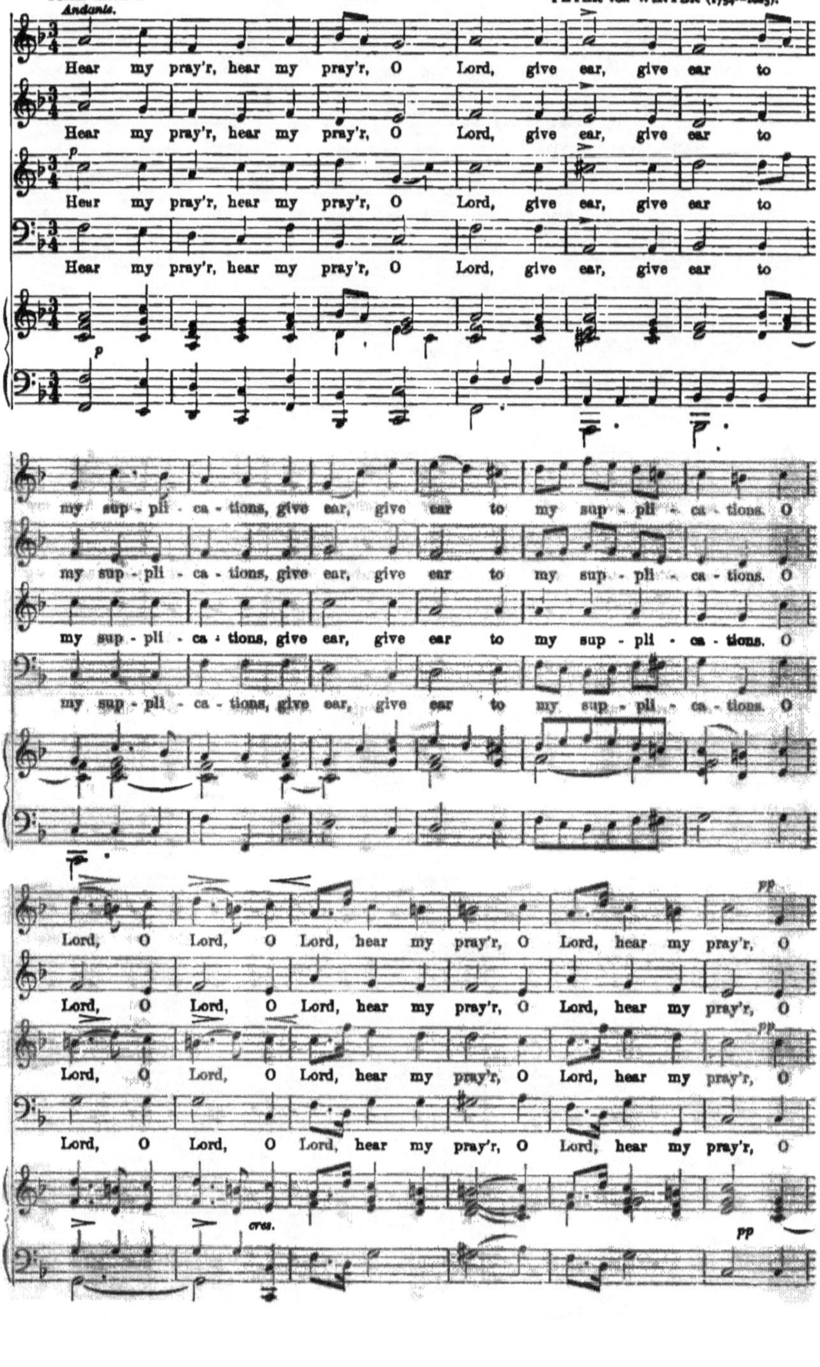

Lord, hear my pray'r, O Lord, hear my pray'r.
Lord, hear my pray'r, O Lord, hear my pray'r. In Thy faith - - ful-
Lord, hear my pray'r, O Lord, hear my pray'r. In Thy faith - - ful-
Lord, hear my pray'r, O Lord, hear my pray'r. In Thy faith - - ful-ness an-swer
mf
an - swer me, and in Thy right - eous - ness. O Lord, hear my
ness an-swer me, and in Thy right - eous - ness. O Lord, hear my
ness an-swer me, and in Thy right - eous - ness. O Lord,
me, an-swer me, and in Thy right - eous - ness. O Lord,
p
dim.   pp
pray'r, hear my pray'r, hear my pray'r, give ear, give ear to my
pray'r, hear my pray'r, hear my pray'r, give ear, give ear to my
hear my pray'r, hear my pray'r, give ear to
hear my pray'r, hear my pray'r, hear my pray'r, give ear to my sup-pli-
p   dim.   pp
pp

cres.
mf
sup - - pli - ca - tion. O Lord, O Lord, O Lord, hear my pray'r,
sup - pli - ca - tion. O Lord, O Lord, O Lord, hear my pray'r,
cres.
mf
my sup - pli - ca - tion. O Lord, O Lord, O Lord, hear my pray'r,
ca - tion. O Lord, O Lord, O Lord, hear my pray'r,
cres.
8ve.
pp dolce.
cres.
give ear, give ear to my sup - pli - ca - tion. O Lord, O Lord,
give ear, give ear to my sup - pli - ca - tion. O Lord, O Lord,
pp
give ear, give ear to my sup - pli - ca - tion. O Lord, O Lord,
give ear, give ear to my sup - pli - ca - tion. O Lord, O Lord,
pp
cres.
mf
pp
O Lord, hear my pray'r, give ear to my sup - pli - ca - tion.
O Lord, hear my pray'r, give ear to my sup - pli - ca - tion.
pp
O Lord, hear my pray'r, give ear to my sup - pli - ca - tion.
O Lord, hear my pray'r, give ear to my sup - pli - ca - tion.
pp

Turn Thy Face from my Sins.

PSALM LI. 9, 10, 11. SIR ARTHUR SEYMOUR SULLIVAN, Mus. D. (1842 —).

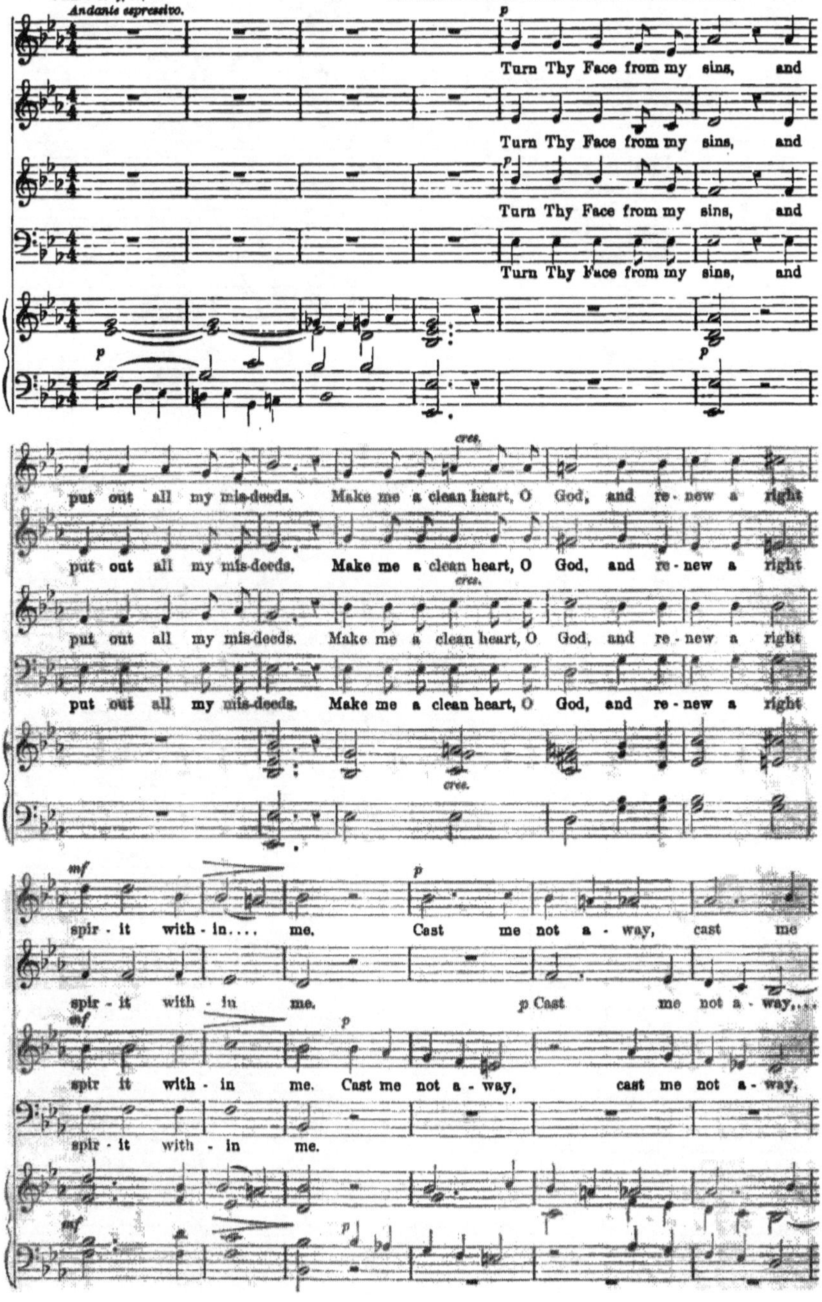

not a - way,.... cast me not a - way from Thy pres - ence; and
...... cast...... me.... not a - way..... from Thy pres - ence;
cast me not a - way from Thy pres - ence;
cast me not a - way from............. Thy pres - ence;
take not Thy Ho - ly Spir - it... from...... me.
and take not Thy Ho - ly Spir - it
Turn Thy Face from my sins, and put out all my mis-
Turn Thy Face from my sins, and put out all my mis-
from me. Turn Thy Face from my sins, and put out all my mis-
Turn Thy Face from my sins, and put out all my mis-

Turn Thy Face from my Sins.

Ave verum.

(JESU, WORD OF GOD INCARNATE.)

Johannes Chrysostomus Wolfgang Theophilus (Gottlieb or Amadeus) Mozart (1756—1791).

Ave verum.

us........... men with nails was torn.
cru - - - ce pro ho - mi - ne.
Cleanse us
Ou - - jus

For us men with nails was torn.
in cru - ce pro ho - mi - ne.
Cleanse us
Cu - jus

For us men with nails was torn.
in cru - ce pro ho - mi - ne.
Cleanse us
Cu - jus

For us men with nails was torn.
in cru - ce pro ho - mi - ne.
Cleanse us
Cu - jus

dim.
p

by the Blood and Wa - ter Stream - ing from Thy pierc - ed Side;
la - tus per - fo - ra - tum un - da flux - it et san - gui - ne.
dim.

by the Blood and Wa - ter Stream - ing from Thy pierc - ed Side;
la - tus per - fo - ra - tum un - da flux - it et san - gui - ne.

by the Blood and Wa - ter Stream - ing from Thy pierc - ed Side;
la - tus per - fo - ra - tum un - da flux - it et san - gui - ne.
dim.

by the Blood and Wa - ter Stream - ing from Thy pierc - ed Side;
la - tus per - fo - ra - tum un - da flux - it et san - gui - ne.

dim.

Feed us with Thy Bod - y brok - en, Now....... and in death's a - go - ny, Now
Es - to no - bis præ - gus - ta - tum in mor - - - - tis ex - a - mi - ne, in
Feed us with Thy Bod - y brok - en, Now....... and in death's a - go - ny,
Es - to no - bis præ - gus - ta - tum in mor - - - - tis ex - a - mi - ne,
Feed us with Thy Bod - - y broken, Now and in death's a - go - ny,
Es - to no - bis præ - gus - ta - tum in mor - tis ex - a - mi - ne,
Feed us with Thy Bod - - y broken, Now and in death's a - go - ny,
Es - to no - bis præ - gus - ta - tum in mor - tis ex - a - mi - ne,
now,....... now, now........ and in death's a - go - ny.
mor - - - - - - - tis ex - a - mi - ne.
Now, now,.................. and in death's a - go - ny.
in mor - - - - tis ex - a - mi - ne.
Now, now,.................. and in death's a - go - ny.
in mor - - - - tis ex - a - mi - ne.
Now, now....... and in death's a - go - ny,
in mor - - - - - tis ex - a - mi - ne.

Ave verum.
(JESU, WORD OF GOD INCARNATE.)

CHARLES FRANCOIS GOUNOD (1818 ——).

NOTE.—Should this Motett be accompanied, the first seven measures may be played, and the voices commence at the eighth measure.

Sa - cred Bod - y For us men with nails was torn; Cleanse us by the
im - mo - la - tum In cru - ce pro ho - mi - ne; Cu - jus la - tus
Sa - cred Bod - y For us men with nails was torn; Cleanse us by the
im - mo - la - tum In cru - ce pro ho - mi - ne; Cu - jus la - tus
Sa - cred Bod - y For us men with nails was torn; Cleanse us by the
im - mo - la - tum In cru - ce pro ho - mi - ne; Cu - jus la - tus
Sa - cred Bod - y For us men with nails was torn; Cleanse us by the
im - mo - la - tum In cru - ce pro ho - mi - ne; Cu - jus la - tus
Blood and Wa - ter stream - ing from Thy pierc - ed side, Feed us with Thy
per - fo - ra - tum flu - xit un - da et san - gui - ne, Es - to no - bis
Blood and Wa - ter stream - ing from Thy pierc - ed side, Feed us with Thy
per - fo - ra - tum flu - xit un - da et san - gui - ne, Es - to no - bis
Blood and Wa - ter stream - ing from Thy pierc - ed side, Feed us with Thy
per - fo - ra - tum flu - xit un - da et san - gui - ne, Es - to no - bis
Blood and Wa - ter stream - ing from Thy pierc - ed side, Feed us with Thy
per - fo - ra - tum flu - xit un - da et san - gui - ne, Es - to no - bis

Ave verum.

cres. molto. f p p
Bod-y brok-en Now and in death's a-go-ny. O Je-su, hear us,
prae-gus-ta-tum Mor-tis in ex-a-mi-ne. O Je-su dul-cis,

Bod-y brok-en Now and in death's a-go-ny. O Je-su, hear us,
prae-gus-ta-tum Mor-tis in ex-a-mi-ne. O Je-su dul-cis,

cres. molto. f p p
Bod-y brok-en Now and in death's a-go-ny. O Je-su, hear us,
prae-gus-ta-tum Mor-tis in ex-a-mi-ne. O Je-su dul-cis,

Bod-y brok-en Now and in death's a-go-ny, O Je-su, hear us, O
prae-gus-ta-tum Mor-tis in ex-a-mi-ne. O Je-su dul-cis, O

cres. molto. f p p

cres. f p
O Je-su, spare us; Je-su, Je-su, Son.... of Ma-ry, O grant us, Lord, Thy
O Je-su pi-e, Je-su, Je-su, fi-li Ma-ri-a, In no-bis mi-se-

O Je-su, spare us; Je-su, Je-su, Son.... of Ma-ry, O grant us, Lord, Thy
O Je-su pi-e, Je-su, Je-su, fi-li Ma-ri-a, In no-bis mi-se-

cres. p
O Je-su, spare us; Je-su, Je-su, Son.... of Ma-ry, O grant us, Lord, Thy
O Je-su pi-e, Je-su, Je-su, fi-li Ma-ri-a, In no-bis mi-se-

Je-su, spare us; Je-su, Je-su, Son.... of Ma-ry, O grant us, Lord, Thy
Je-su pi-e, Je-su, Je-su, fi-li Ma-ri-a, In no-bis mi-se-

cres. f p

Ave verum.

mer - cy, O grant us, Lord, Thy mer - cy, O grant us, O grant us, Lord, Thy mer -
re - re, In no - bis mi - se - re - re, O Je - su, In no - bis mi - se - re -

mer - cy, O grant us, Lord, Thy mer - cy, O grant us, O grant us, Lord, Thy mer -
re - re, In no - bis mi - se - re - re, O Je - su, In no - bis mi - se - re -

mer - cy, O grant us, Lord, Thy mer - cy, O grant us, O grant us, Lord, Thy mer -
re - re, In no - bis mi - se - re - re, O Je - su, In no - bis mi - se - re -

mer - cy, O grant us, Lord, Thy mer - cy, O grant us, O grant us, Lord, Thy mer -
re - re, In no - bis mi - se - re - re, O Je - su, In no - bis mi - se - re -

cy.... A - men! A - men! A - men! A - men!
re.... A - men! A - men! A - men! A - men!

cy.... A - men! A - men! A - men! A - men!
re.... A - men! A - men! A - men! A - men!

cy.... A - men! A - men! A - men! A - men!
re.... A - men! A - men! A - men! A - men!

cy. A - - men! A - - men! A - - men!..... A - men!
re. A - - men! A - - men! A - - men!..... A - men!

Remember not, Lord, our Offences.

Andante. ♩ = 88. HENRY PURCELL (1658—1695.)

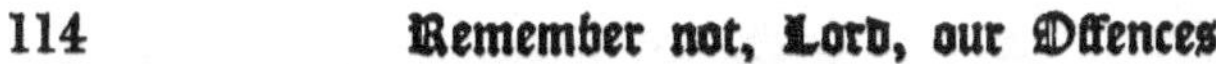

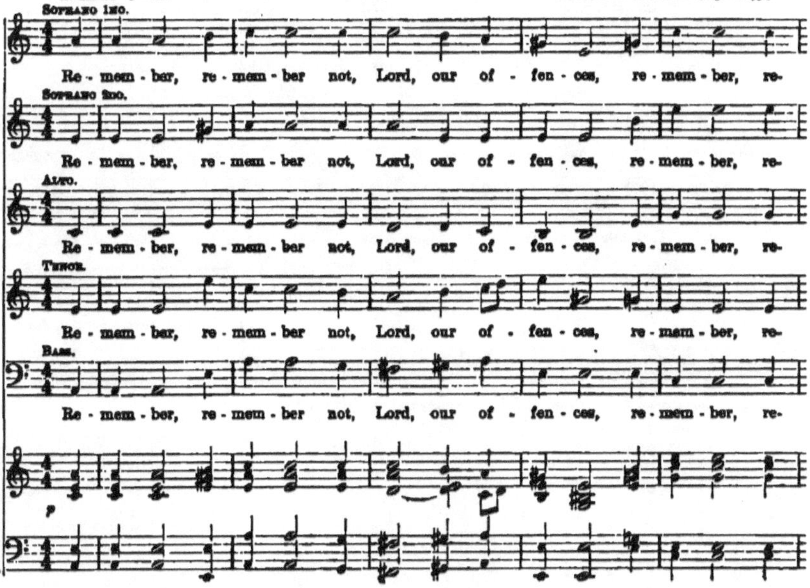

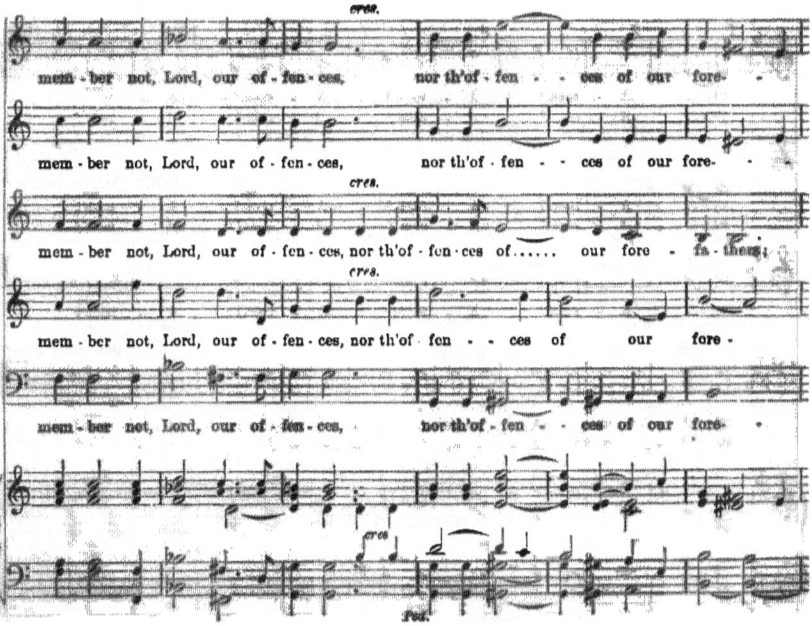

fa - thers; nei - - ther take Thou vengeance of our sins,
fa - thers; but spare........ us, good Lord, nei - ther take Thou vengeance
nei - ther take Thou vengeance of our sins, but spare......
fa - thers; nei - - ther take Thou vengeance of our
fa - thers; nei - - ther take Thou vengeance of our sins.
nei - - ther take Thou vengeance of our sins, but spare...... us, good
of our sins, good Lord, nei - ther take Thou vengeance
- us, good Lord, nei - ther take Thou vengeance of our sins,
sins, good Lord, good Lord, nei - ther take Thou
but spare........ us, good Lord, nei -

Lord, nei - - - ther take Thou vengeance of our sins, but spare....... us, good
of our sins, nei - - ther take thou vengeance of our sins,
nei - - ther take Thou ven-geance of our sins good........... Lord, but spare....
vengeance of our sins, but spare...... us, good Lord,
- - ther take Thou vengeance of our sins, but

Lord, spare........ us, good Lord, spare Thy peo - ple, whom Thou hast re -
but spare........ us, good Lord, spare Thy peo - ple, whom Thou hast re -
.... us, spare........ us, good Lord, spare Thy peo - ple, whom Thou hast re -
but spare us, good.... Lord, spare Thy peo - ple, whom Thou hast re -
spare us, good Lord, spare Thy peo - ple, whom Thou hast re -

deem-ed with Thy pre - - cious Blood, and be not an-gry with us for - ev -
deem-ed with Thy pre - cious Blood, and be not an-gry with us for ev -
deem-ed with Thy pre - - cious Blood, and be not an-gry with us for ev -
deem-ed with Thy pre - - cious Blood, and be not an-gry with us for ev -
deem-ed with Thy pre - - cious Blood, and be not an-gry with us for ev -
er, be not an-gry with us for - ev - - er. Spare us, good Lord.
er, be not an-gry with us for - ev - - er. Spare us, good Lord.
er, be not an-gry with us for - ev - - er. Spare us, good Lord.
er, be not an-gry with us for - ev - - er. Spare us, good Lord.
er, be not an-gry with us for - ev - - er. Spare us, good Lord.

O Saviour of the World.

FROM THE OFFICE FOR THE VISITATION OF THE SICK.

Sir JOHN GOSS, Mus. D. (1800—1880).

world, O Sav-iour, Who by Thy Cross and precious Blood hast re-deem-ed us, Save us, and
world, O Sav-iour, Who by Thy Cross and precious Blood hast re-deem-ed us, Save us, and
world, O Sav-iour, Who by Thy Cross and precious Blood hast re-deem-ed us, Save us, and
world, O Sav-iour, Who by Thy Cross and precious Blood hast re-deem-ed us,
help us, we hum-bly be-seech Thee, O Lord, we hum-bly be-seech Thee, O
help us, we hum-bly be-seech Thee, O Lord, we hum-bly be-seech Thee, O
help us, we hum-bly be-seech Thee, O Lord, we hum-bly beseech Thee, be-seech Thee, O
help us, we hum-bly be-seech Thee, O Lord, we hum-bly be-seech Thee, O
Lord, O Sav-iour of the world, O Sav-iour of the
Lord, O Sav-iour of the world, O Sav-iour of the
Lord, O Sav-iour of the world, O.
Lord, O Sav-iour of the world, O save us, and help

O Saviour of the World.

Why seek ye the Living among the Dead.

Why seek ye the Living among the Dead.

liv-er-ed in-to the hands of sin-ful men, and be cru-ci-fied, and be
and be cru-ci-fied, and be
and be cru-ci-fied, and be
liv-er-ed in-to the hands of sin-ful men, and be cru-ci-fied, and be
Ped.
f
cru-ci-fied, and the third day rise a-gain.
cru-ci-fied, and the third day rise a-gain. The Son of Man must be de-
dim.
f
cru-ci-fied, and the third day rise a-gain. The Son of Man must be de-
cru-ci-fied, and the third day rise a-gain.
f
No Ped.
and be cru - ci -
liv-er-ed in-to the hands of sin-ful men, and be cru-ci-fied, and be
liv-er-ed in-to the hands of sin-ful men, and be cru-ci-fied, and be
and be cru-ci-fied, and be
Ped.

Why seek ye the Living among the Dead.

rise...... a - gain, and the third day rise a - gain, the third day rise a-
rise...... a - gain, and the third day rise a - gain, the
.... a - gain, and the third day rise a - gain,
rise...... a - gain, and the third day.. rise a - gain, the third day
- gain, the third day rise a - gain, the third day rise... a-
third day rise a - gain, the third day rise...... rise...... a-
rise a - gain, the third day rise, rise a-
rise a - gain, rise a - gain, rise, rise a-
gain. He is not here, but is ris - en.
gain. He is not here, but is ris - en.
gain. He is not here, but is ris - en.
gain. He is not here, but is ris - en.
ff
ff
ff

Christ our Passover is sacrificed for us.

but with th'unleavened bread of sin-cer-i-ty, th'unleavened bread of sin-cer-i-ty and truth.
CHORUS—Time as at first.
Christ.. our Pass-o-ver is sac-ri-fic-ed for us, there-fore let us keep the
Christ.. our Pass-o-ver is sac-ri-fic-ed for us, there-fore let us keep the
Christ.. our Pass-o-ver is sac-ri-fic-ed for us, there-fore let us keep the
Christ.. our Pass-o-ver is sac-ri-fic-ed for us, there-fore let us keep the
feast, there-fore let us keep the feast; Not with the old leaven, nor with the leav-en of
feast, therefore let us keep the feast; Not with the old leaven, nor with the leaven of
feast, therefore let us keep the feast; Not.. with the old leaven, nor with the leaven of
feast, there-fore let us keep the feast; Not with the old leaven, nor with the leaven of

Christ our Passover is sacrificed for us.

1 COR. XV. 20; ROMANS VI. 10.
SIR GEORGE JOB ELVEY, MUS. D. (1816 ——).
Christ is ris - en from the dead, is ris - - - - en, Christ is
Christ is ris - en from the dead, Christ is ris - - en, Christ is
Christ is ris - en.... from the dead, Christ.... is ris - en,.... Christ.. is
Christ is ris - en from the dead, Christ is ris - en, Christ is ris - en, Christ is
ris - en from the dead, Al - le - lu - ia, Al - le - lu - ia. Christ is ris - en
ris - en from the dead, Al - le - lu - ia, Al - le - lu - ia. Christ is ris - en
ris - en from the dead, Al - le - lu - ia, Al - le - lu - ia. Christ is ris - en.
ris - en from the dead, Al - le - lu - ia, Al - le - lu - ia. Christ is ris - en
from the dead, is ris - en from the dead, Christ.... is ris - en from...... the dead.
from the dead, Christ is ris - en from the dead, is ris - en from the dead.
..... from the dead, Christ is ris - en from the dead, is ris - en from the dead.
from the dead, Christ is ris - en from the dead, is ris - en from the dead.

Christ is risen from the Dead.

God, He liv-eth, liv - eth..... un-to God, He liv - - eth, liveth un -
liv - - eth, He liv - eth un - to God, He liv - eth, liv - eth
liv-eth un - to God, He liv - eth.... un-to God, He liv-eth, liv - eth
liv-eth un-to God, He liv - eth un - to God, He liv-eth, liv - eth
- - to God. Christ.... is ris - en from the dead, Al-le-lu-ia, Al-le-lu-ia,
un - to God. Christ is ris - en from the dead, Al-le-lu-ia, Al-le-lu-ia,
un - to God. Christ is ris - en.... from the dead, Al-le-lu-ia, Al-le-lu-ia,
un - to God. Christ is ris - en from the dead, Al-le-lu-ia, Al-le-lu-ia,
Al-le-lu-ia, Al-le-lu-ia, Al - le - lu - ia,
Al-le-lu-ia, Al-le-lu-ia, Al - le - lu - ia,
Al-le-lu-ia, Al-le-lu-ia, Al - le - lu - ia,
Al-le-lu-ia, Al-le-lu-ia, Al-le-- lu - ia,

God hath appointed a Day.

ACTS XVII. 31 ; Ps. LXXXV. 10 ; 1 COR. XV. 57.
BERTHOLD TOURS (1838 ——), 1878.

CHORUS. marcato.
f
men, in......... that He hath rais - ed Him, hath rais - ed Him from the
in......... that He hath rais - ed Him, hath rais - ed Him from the
f
in......... that He hath rais - ed Him, hath rais - ed Him from the
in......... that He hath rais - ed Him, hath rais - ed Him from the
f
Ped. ff
ff
rallentando.
dead,................ hath rais - ed Him from the dead.........
dead,................ hath rais - ed Him from the dead.........
ff
rallentando.
dead,................ hath rais - ed Him from the dead.........
dead,................ hath rais - ed Him from the dead.........
ff marcato.
rallentando.
Andante tranquillo. ♩ = 68.
p

God hath appointeth a Day.

SOLO. p
Righteousness and peace have kiss-ed each
SOLO. mf
Righteousness and peace have kissed each oth - er,
oth - er, Righteousness and peace have kiss-ed each oth - er, Righteousness and
SOLO.
Righteousness and peace have kiss-ed each oth - er, Righteousness and
Righteousness and peace have kiss-ed each oth - er, Righteousness and
SOLO.
Right - eous - ness... and peace have kiss - ed each oth - - -
peace have kiss-ed each oth - er... Mer-cy and truth,.... mer-cy and
peace have kiss-ed each oth - er... Mer-cy and truth,.... mer-cy and
peace have kiss-ed each oth - er... Mer-cy and truth,.... mer-cy and
er, each oth - - er...... Mer-cy and truth,.... mer-cy and
poco cres.
p
poco cres.
p
poco cres.
pp
dim. poco ritard. pp CHORUS—a tempo.
dim. poco ritard. pp
dim. poco rit. pp a tempo.

God hath appointed a Day.

Allegro. ♩ = 76.
pp
pp
Thanks be to God,
thanks be to God,
Thanks be to God,
thanks be to God,
pp
pp
Thanks be to God,
thanks be to God,
Thanks be to God,
thanks be to God,
mf poco marcato.
(Voices alone.)
mf
(Voices alone.)
f molto marcato.
ff
thanks be to God,
thanks be to God,
ff
thanks be to God,
thanks be to God,
ff
Ped.
dim.
Allegro con spirito. ♩ = 88. f marcato.
thanks be to God,
Thanks be to God, Which
thanks be to God,
Thanks be to God, Which
dim.
f marcato.
thanks be to God,
Thanks be to God, Which
thanks be to God.
Thanks be to God, Which
f marcato.

giv-eth us the vic-to-ry, thanks be to God, Which giv-eth us the vic-to-ry,
giv-eth us the vic-to-ry, thanks be to God, Which giv-eth us the vic-to-ry,
giv-eth us the vic-to-ry, thanks be to God, Which giv-eth us the vic-to-ry,
giv-eth us the vic-to-ry, thanks be to God, Which giv-eth us the vic-to-ry,
ff
thanks be to God, thanks be to God, thanks be to God,
thanks be to God, thanks be to God, thanks be to God,
ff
thanks be to God, thanks be to God, thanks be to God,
thanks be to God, thanks be to God, thanks be to God,
ff
SOLO, mf
thanks be to God, Which giv-eth us the vic-to-ry through our Lord Je-sus
thanks be to God, Which giv-eth us the vic-to-ry through our Lord Je-sus
mf
thanks be to God, Which giv-eth us the vic-to-ry through our Lord Je-sus
thanks be to God, Which giv-eth us the vic-to-ry through our Lord Je-sus
(Voices alone.)

CHORUS. f
Christ, Thanks be to God, Which giv - eth us the vic - to - ry, thanks be to
Christ. Thanks be to God, Which giv - eth us the vic - to - ry, thanks be to
Christ. Thanks be to God, Which giv - eth us the vic - to - ry, thanks be to
Christ. Thanks be to God, Which giv - eth us the vic - to - ry, thanks be to
Org. f
God, Which giveth us the vic - to - ry, Which giveth us the vic - to - ry, Which giv-eth us the
God, Which giveth us the vic - to - ry, Which giveth us the vic - to - ry, Which giv-eth us the
God, Which giveth us the vic - to - ry, Which giveth us the vic - to - ry, the
God, Which giveth us the vic - to - ry, Which giveth us the vic - to - ry, the
vic - to - ry, Which giv - eth us the
vic - to - ry, Which giv - eth us the
vic - to - ry, Which giv - eth us, Which giv - eth
vic - to - ry, Which giv - eth

 God hath appointed a Day

vic - to - ry. A - - - - men, A - - men,...
vic - to - ry. A - - - men, A - - men,...
vic - to ry. A - - - men, A - - men,...
vic - to - ry. A - - - - - - men,
A - - men,..... A - - - men, Which giv - eth us the
A - - - - - - men, A - - men, Which giv - eth us the
A - - - men, A - - - men, Which giv - eth us the
A - - - - - men, A - - men, Which giv - eth us the
vic - to - ry through our Lord Je - sus Christ. A - men.
vic - to - ry through our Lord Je - sus.... Christ. A - men.
vic - to - ry through our Lord Je - sus.... Christ. A - men.
vic - to - ry through our Lord Je - sus Christ. A - men.
vic - to - ry through our Lord Je - sus.... Christ. A - men.
ff a tempo.
sempre ff
ri - - tar - - dan - - do. Adagio. ff
ri - tar - dan - do. Adagio. ff

Christ is risen from the Dead.

glad and re - joice in His sal - va - tion.
glad and re - joice in His sal - va - tion.
glad and re - joice in His sal - va - tion.
glad and re - joice in His sal - va - tion.
Christ is ris - en!
Christ is ris - en!
Al - le - lu - ia!
Al - le - lu - ia!
He is the First - be-gotten of the
He is the First - be-gotten of the
and the Prince...... of the kings of the earth.
dead, and the Prince of the kings of the earth.
legato.

Christ is risen from the Dead.

Him That lov - ed us, and washed us from our sins in His Own
Him That lov - ed us, and washed us from our sins in His Own
Un - to Him That lov - ed us, and washed us,
Him That lov - ed us, and washed us from our
Blood, and hath made us kings and priests un - to God and His
Blood, and hath made us kings and priests un - to God and His
washed us from our sins in His Own Blood, and hath made us kings and
sins, and hath made us kings and priests un - to God and His
Fa - ther, To Him be glo - ry, be glo - ry and do-
Fa - ther, To Him be glo - ry, To Him be glo - ry and do-
priests un - to God, To Him be glo - ry, To Him be glo - ry and do-
Fa - ther, To Him be glo - ry, be glo - - -

min - ion, for - ev - er, be glo - ry and do - min - ion for -
min - ion, To Him be glo - ry for - ev - er, be glo - ry for -
min - ion, To Him be glo - ry for - ev - er, be glo - ry and do -
ry, for - ev - er, be glo - ry and do - min - ion for -
f dim. p ac - cel - e - ran - do.
ev - er. A - men, A -
ev - er. A - men, A -
dim. p ac - cel - e - ran - do.
min - ion for - ev - er. A - men, A -
ev - er. A - men, A -
ac - cel - e - ran - do.
ff
f dim. rall. molto. p pp
men. A - men.
men. A - men.
f dim. rall. molto. p pp
men. A - men.
men. A - men.
rall. molto. a tempo.
ff

Romans vi. 9.
Andante.
Sir GEORGE JOB ELVEY, Mus. D. (1816 ——).
Christ be-ing rais-ed from the dead, Christ be-ing rais-ed
Christ be-ing rais-ed from the dead, Christ be-ing rais-ed
Christ be-ing rais-ed from the dead, Christ be-ing rais-ed
Christ be-ing rais-ed from the dead, Christ be-ing rais-ed
8ves. sempre con Ped.
from the dead, Christ be-ing rais-ed from the
from the dead, Christ be-ing rais - - ed from the
from the dead, Christ be-ing rais-ed from the
from the dead, Christ be-ing rais-ed rais - - ed from the
dead, di-eth no more, di-
dead, di-eth no more, di - - eth no more, di-
dead, di-eth no more, di - - eth no
dead, di-eth no more, di - - eth no more,

Christ being raised from the Dead.

o - ver Him, Death hath no more, no more do - min - ion o - ver
o - ver Him, Death hath no more, no more do - min - ion o - ver
o - ver Him, Death hath no more, no more do - min - ion o - ver
o - ver Him, Death hath no more,... no more.... do - min - ion o - ver
pp
Him, Death hath no more do - min - ion o - ver Him, no more do-
Him, Death hath no more do - min - ion o - ver Him, no more do-
Him, Death hath no more do - min - ion o - ver Him, no more do-
Him, Death hath no more do - min - ion o - ver Him, no more do-
ff
min - - ion o - - ver Him.
min - - ion o - ver Him.
min - - ion o - - ver Him.
min - - ion o - - ver Him.

O Risen Lord!

ALFRED BELL.
Allegro moderato. ♩ = 92.
JOSEPH BARNBY (1838 —.)
f
cres - cen - - - do.
ritenuto.
ff
a tempo
O ris - en Lord! O Christ as - cend - ed! O Prince of
O ris - en Lord! O Christ as - cend - ed! O Prince of
O ris - en Lord! O Christ as - cend - ed! O Prince of
O ris - en Lord! O Christ as - cend - ed! O Prince of
Peace! Thy toils on earth are end - ed, and Thou art on Thy ev - er - last - ing throne a-
Peace! Thy toils on earth are end - ed, and Thou art on Thine ev - er - last - ing throne a-
Peace! Thy toils on earth are end - ed, and Thou art on Thine ev - er - last - ing throne a-
Peace! Thy toils on earth are end - ed, and Thou art on Thine ev - er - last - ing throne a-

dor'd. O hear our songs, O hear our pray'rs and prais-es, O grant us peace,
dor'd. O hear our songs, O hear our pray'rs and prais-es, O grant us peace,
dor'd. O hear.. our songs, O hear our pray'rs and prais-es, O grant us peace,
dor'd. O hear our pray'rs and prais-es, O grant us peace,
grant us peace. Thy pil-grim church still rais - es Her ar-dent gaze to Thee, As
grant us peace. Her ar-dent gaze to Thee, As
grant us peace. Thy church her gaze still rais - es to Thee, As for Thy
grant us peace. As for Thy rest.
for Thy rest she longs, Thy rest.... she longs, As for Thy rest she longs, Thou, Je-su
for Thy rest, Thy rest she longs, Thy rest she longs, Thou, Je-su
rest, Thy rest she longs, as for Thy rest she longs, Thy rest she longs, Thou, Je-su
.... she longs, Thy rest,.......... Thy rest she longs, Thou, Je-su

O Risen Lord!

King,........ to heav'n as - cend - ing, With gifts of peace Thy pierc-ed palms ex-
King,........ to heav'n as - cend - ing, With gifts of peace...... Thy pierc-ed palms ex-
King, to heav'n as - cend - ing, ... With gifts of peace Thy pierced palms.... ex-
King, to heav'n as - cend - - ing, With gifts Thy palms ex-
tend - ing, shed'st worlds of hope and joy,.. shed'st worlds of hope and joy,.... Thou, Je - su King, as-
tend - ing, shed'st worlds of hope and joy,.. shed'st worlds of hope and joy,.... Thou, Je - su King, as-
tend - ing, shed'st worlds of hope and joy,.. shed'st worlds of hope and joy,.... Thou, Je - su King, as-
tend - ing, shed'st worlds of hope and joy,.. shed'st worlds of hope and joy,.... Thou, Je - su King, as-
cend - ing, shed'st worlds of hope and joy, Thy pierc - ed palms ex - tend ing, Thou, Je - su King, as-
cend - ing, shed'st hope and joy, Thy pierc - ed palms ex - tend - ing, Thou, Je - su King, as-
cend - ing, shed'st hope and joy, Thy pierc - ed palms ex - tend - ing, Thou, Je - su King, as-
cend - ing, shed'st hope and joy, Thy pierc - ed palms ex - tend - ing, Thou, Je - su King, as-

cend - ing, shed'st worlds of hope and joy, shed'st worlds of hope and joy. O ris-en Lord! O Prince of
cend - ing, shed'st worlds of hope and joy, of hope, of hope and joy. O ris-en Lord! O Prince of
cend - ing, shed'st worlds of hope and joy, shed'st worlds of hope, of hope and joy. O risen Lord! O Prince of
cend - ing, shed'st worlds of hope and joy, of hope and joy.
peace, To Thee we sing Al - le - lu - ia, O ris - en Lord! O Prince of peace, To Thee we
peace, To Thee we sing Al - le - lu - ia, O ris - en Lord! O Prince of peace, To Thee we
peace, To Thee we sing Al - le - lu - ia, O ris - en Lord! O Prince of peace, To Thee we
To Thee we sing Al - le - lu - ia, O ris - en Lord! O Prince of peace, To Thee we
sing Al-le-lu - ia. A - - men, A - - men.
sing Al-le-lu - ia. A - - men, A - - men.
sing Al-le-lu - ia, Al-le-lu-ia, Al-le-lu-ia. A - men, Al-le-lu-ia, A - men.
sing Al - le - lu - ia. A - - men. A - - men.

Come, Holy Ghost.

Translated by The Right Rev. JOHN COSIN, D.D.,
Bishop of Durham (1594—1672), 1627.

THOMAS ATTWOOD (1767—1838).

* May be sung as a Solo or by all the Soprani.

* Verse 2 may be sung as a Quartet, and unaccompanied.

Come, Holy Ghost.

* Pause for the last verse only.

In humble Faith and holy Love.

The Very Rev. THOMAS RENNELL, D.D. (1753—1840).   GEORGE MURSELL GARRETT, Mus. D. (1834 —).

VERSE. *Andante. Very smooth. p*

In humble Faith and holy Love.

In humble Faith and holy Love.

In humble Faith and holy Love.

faith and love; Till God His vis-ion shall be-stow, In Christ's tri-
Till God His vis-ion shall be-stow, In Christ's tri-
Till God His vis-ion shall be-stow, In Christ's tri-
Till God His vis-ion shall be-stow, In Christ's tri-
umph-ant Church a-bove. To God our
umph-ant Church a-bove. To God our
umph-ant Church a-bove. To God our
umph-ant Church a-bove. To God our
Fa-ther raise the voice, In-vi-si-
Fa-ther raise the voice, In-vi-si-

In humble Faith and holy Love.

Grant to us, Lord, we beseech Thee.

The Collect for the Ninth Sunday after Trinity.

JOSEPH BARNBY (1838 —).

Grant to us, Lord, we beseech Thee.

live ac-cord-ing to Thy Word, May by Thee be en-
live ac-cord-ing to Thy Word, May by Thee be en-
Word, ac-cord-ing to Thy Word, May by Thee be en-a-bled to
cord-ing to Thy Word, May by Thee be en-
a-bled to live ac-cord-ing to Thy Word, through
a-bled to live ac-cord-ing to Thy Word, through
live, to live ac-cord-ing to Thy Word, through
a-bled to live ac-cord-ing to Thy Word, through
Je-sus Christ our Lord, through Je-sus Christ our Lord. A-men.....
Je-sus Christ our Lord, through Je-sus Christ our Lord. A-men.....
Je-sus Christ our Lord, through Je-sus Christ our Lord. A-men.....
Je-sus Christ our Lord, through Je-sus Christ our Lord. A-men.....

Almighty and Merciful God.

Sir JOHN GOSS, Mus. D. (1800—1880).

fail not fi-nal-ly to at-tain Thy heav'n - ly prom-is-es; through the mer-its of
fail not fi-nal-ly to at-tain Thy heav'n - ly prom-is-es; through the mer-its of
fail not fi-nal-ly to at-tain........ Thy heav'nly prom-is-es; through the mer-its of
fail not fi-nal-ly to at-tain Thy heav'n - ly prom-is-es; through the mer-its of
Je - sus Christ, through the mer-its of Je - sus Christ, thro' the mer-its of
Je - sus Christ, thro' the mer-its, the mer-its of Christ, thro' the mer-its, thro' the mer-its of
Je - sus Christ, thro' the mer-its of Christ, thro' the mer-its of Christ, thro' the
Je - sus Christ, thro' the mer-its of Je - - - sus Christ, thro' the mer-its of
Je - sus Christ our Lord........... A - - - men......
Je - sus Christ........ our Lord. A - - - - men.
mer-its of Je - sus Christ our Lord. A - - - - - men.
Je - sus Christ our Lord. A - men................ A - men.

Lord, we pray Thee.

CHORUS.
Lord, we pray Thee, Lord, we pray Thee that Thy grace may always prevent and follow us, that Thy
Lord, we pray Thee, Lord, we pray Thee that Thy grace may always prevent and follow us,
Lord, we pray Thee, Lord, we pray Thee that Thy grace may always prevent and follow us,
Lord, we pray Thee, Lord, we pray Thee that Thy grace may always prevent and follow us,
p a tempo.
grace may al-ways pre-vent and fol-low us, and make us con-tin-ual-ly, and make us con-
may al-ways pre-vent and fol-low us, and make us con-tin-ual-
may al-ways pre-vent and fol-low us, and make us con-
may al-ways pre-vent and fol-low us, and
tin-ual-ly to be giv'n to all good works; thro' Je-sus Christ our Lord. A-men.
ly...... to be giv'n to all good works; thro' Je-sus Christ our Lord. A-men.
tin-ual-ly to be giv'n to all good works; thro' Je-sus Christ our Lord. A-men.
make us to be giv'n to all good works; thro' Je-sus Christ our Lord. A-men.

Rejoice in the Lord.

Psalm xxxiii. 1, 2.

Sir GEORGE JOB ELVEY, Mus. D. (1816 —).

ful. Praise the Lord with harp, Praise the Lord with harp,
ful. Praise the Lord with harp, Praise the Lord with harp,
ful. Praise the Lord with harp, Praise the Lord with harp,
ful. Praise the Lord with harp, Praise the Lord with harp,
f
p
Sing prais-es un-to Him, sing prais-es un-to Him, sing prais-es un-to
Sing prais-es un-to Him, sing prais-es un-to Him, sing prais-es un-to
Sing prais-es un-to Him, sing prais-es un-to Him,
Sing prais-es un-to Him, sing prais-es un-to Him, sing
f
Him, un-to Him with the lute and in-strument of ten strings. Praise the Lord with
Him, un-to Him with the lute and in-strument of ten strings. Praise the Lord with
un - - to Him with the lute and in-strument of ten strings. Praise the Lord with
prais-es un-to Him with the lute and in-strument of ten strings. Praise the Lord with

Rejoice in the Lord.

The Lord is in His holy Temple.

Habakkuk II. s.

JOHN HENRY CORNELL (1828 ——), 1880.

Adagio. ♩ = 80.

The Lord is in His holy Temple.

ff
The Lord.... is in His ho - ly tem - ple,
The Lord... is in His ho - ly tem - ple,
ff
The Lord... is in His ho - ly tem - ple,
The Lord.... is in His ho - ly tem - ple,
ff
Grt. ff
Ped.
mf
Choir. p
Ped. p
p
let all the earth keep si - lence, si - lence, keep si - lence be - fore Him, let
let all the earth keep si - lence, si - lence, keep si - lence be - fore.. Him, let
p
let all the earth keep si - lence, si - lence, keep si - lence be - fore Him, let
let all the earth keep si - lence, si - lence, keep si - lence be - fore Him, let
rall. molto e dim.
all the earth keep si - lence, keep si - lence be - fore Him.
all the earth keep si - lence, keep si - lence be - fore Him.
rall. molto e dim.
all the earth keep si - lence, keep si - lence be - fore Him.
all the earth keep si - lence, keep si - lence be - fore Him.
rall. molto e dim.
Sw. pp
Ped. pp

I will sing of Thy Power.

.... in the morn - - ing, in the morn - - - ing.
times in the morn - - ing, the morn - - ing.
- - - ing, and will praise Thy mer - cy.
mer - cy be - times.... in the morn - - ing. I will
and will
I will sing, will sing of 'Thy pow'r, O God,
sing of Thy pow'r,..........
praise Thy mer - - - cy be - times in the
and will praise, will praise Thy mer - - - cy in the
and will praise, will praise Thy
and will praise, will praise Thy mer - - - cy be - times in the

12

 # I will sing of Thy Power.

and will praise Thy mer-
I will sing of Thy pow'r, and will praise Thy mer-
and will praise Thy mer-
I will sing of Thy pow'r, and will praise Thy mer-
-cy be-times...... in the morn - - ing.
-cy be-times...... in the morn - - ing.
-cy be-times...... in the morn - - ing.
-cy be-times...... in the morn - - ing.
SOLO—Tenor or Soprano. Andante. ♩ = 76.
For Thou hast been my de-fence and ref - uge in the day of my trou - ble, my de-

I will sing of Thy Power.

CHORUS. Vivace.
Un-to Thee, O my strength, will I sing,........
Un-to Thee, O my strength, will I sing,........
Un-to Thee, O my strength, will I sing,........
Un-to Thee, O my strength, will I sing,........
Un-to Thee, O my strength, will I sing, un-to Thee, O my
Un-to Thee, O my strength, will I sing, un-to Thee, O my
Un-to Thee, O my strength, will I sing, un-to Thee, O my
Un-to Thee, O my strength, will I sing, un-to Thee, O my
strength, un-to Thee, O my strength, will I sing, un-to Thee, O my
strength, un-to Thee, O my strength, will I sing,
strength, un-to Thee, O my strength, will I sing,
strength, un to Thee, O my strength, will I sing, un-to Thee, O my strength, will I sing,

I will sing of Thy Power.

God, art my ref-uge and my mer-ci-ful God,
Thou, O God, art my
God, art my ref-uge and my mer-ci-ful God,
Thou, O God, art my
God, art my ref-uge and my mer-ci-ful God,
Thou, O God, art my
God, art my ref-uge and my mer-ci-ful God,
Thou, O God, art my
ff
ref-uge and mer-ci-ful God,
For Thou, O God, art my
ref-uge and mer-ci-ful God,
For Thou, O God, art my
ref-uge and mer-ci-ful God,
For Thou, O God, art my
ref-uge and mer-ci-ful God,
For Thou, O God, art my
ff
ref-uge...... and........... my mer-ci-ful God, A-men.
ref-uge...... and......... my mer-ci-ful God. A-men.
ref-uge...... and........... my mer-ci-ful God. A-men.
ref-uge...... and........... my mer-ci-ful God. A-men.
rit.

O taste and see how gracious the Lord is.

Psalm xxxiv. 8—11.

Sir ARTHUR SEYMOUR SULLIVAN, Mus. D. (1842 ——).

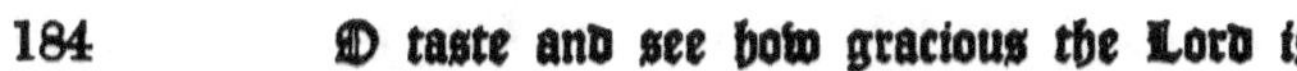

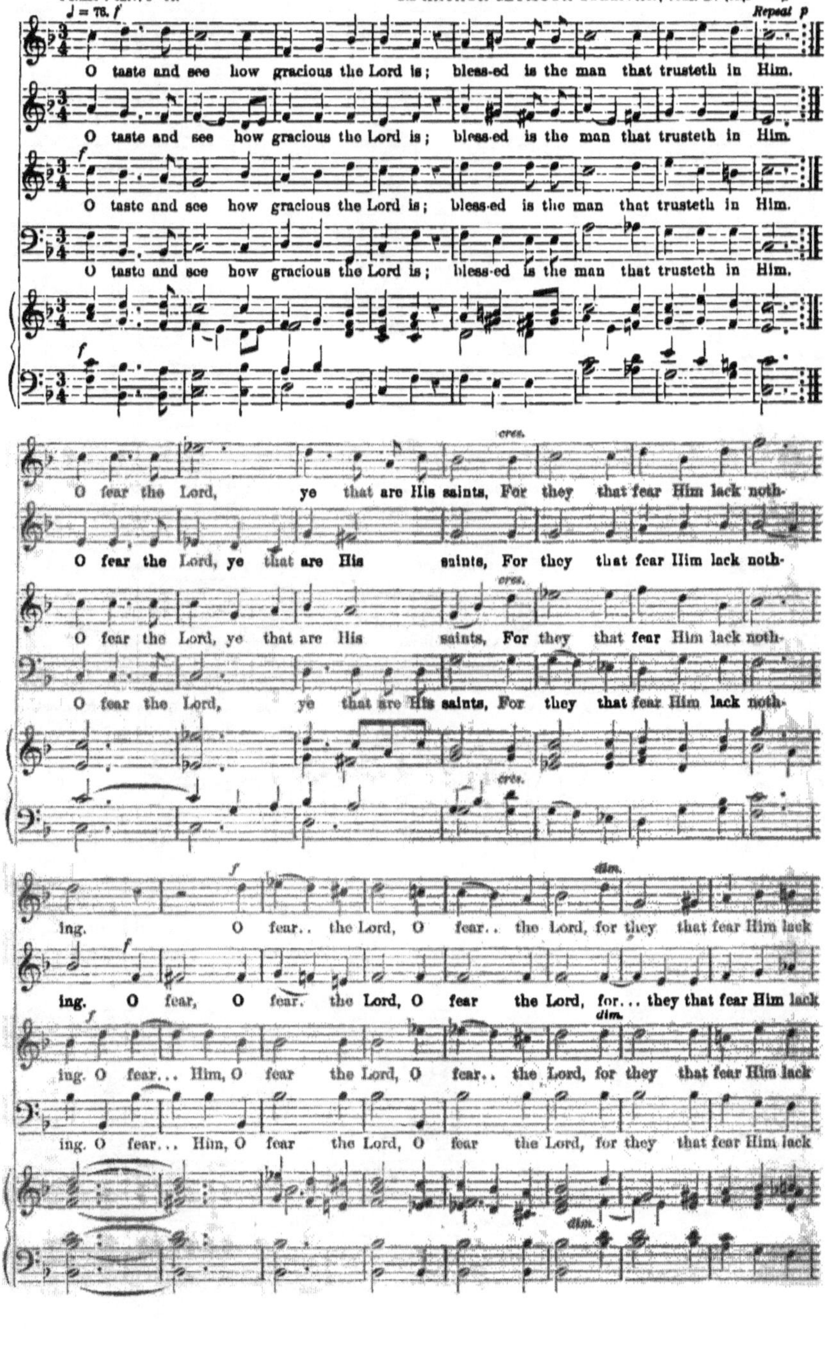

noth - ing.
But they who seek the
noth - ing.
But they who
noth - ing. The li - ons do lack and suf - fer hun-ger,
noth - ing. The li - ons do lack and suf - fer hun-ger,
f dim.
dim.
f
dim.
Lord, who seek the Lord shall want no man-ner of thing that is good.........
seek the Lord, the Lord, shall want no man-ner of thing that is good.........
But they who seek the Lord shall want no man-ner of thing that is good.........
But they who seek the Lord shall want no man - - ner of thing that is good.
p
p
p
I will teach,.......
I will
Come, ye chil - dren, and heark- en un - to me,........
I will
Come, ye chil - dren, and heark- en un - to me,........
I will
f
p
dim.

p
.... you the fear of the Lord. Come, ye chil-dren, and
teach you the fear of the Lord.
teach you the fear of the Lord.
teach you the fear of the Lord.
dolce.
heark - en un - to me.
p
I will teach you the fear
p
I will teach you the fear
pp
rall.
I will teach you the fear..... of the Lord.
of the Lord, I will teach you the fear..... of the Lord.
pp
rall.
of the Lord, I will teach you the fear..... of the Lord.
I will teach you the fear..... of the Lord.
pp

Ps. CXXXV. 1, 2, 3, 19, 20.
Animato. ♩ = 80.
Sir JOHN GOSS, Mus. D. (1800—1880).
O praise the Lord, laud ye the Name of the Lord; praise it, O ye
O praise the Lord, laud ye the Name of the Lord; praise it, O ye
O praise the Lord, laud ye the Name of the Lord; praise it, O ye
O praise the Lord, laud ye the Name of the Lord; praise it, O ye
serv - ants.. of the Lord. Ye that
serv - ants.. of the Lord. Ye that
serv - ants.. of the Lord. Ye that stand in the house of the Lord, that
serv - ants.. of the Lord. Ye that stand in the house of the Lord, that
stand in the house of the Lord,... in the courts of the house of our Lord,
stand in the house of the Lord,... in the courts of the house of our Lord,
stand in the house of the Lord,... in the courts of the house of our Lord,
stand in the house of the Lord,... in the courts of the house of our Lord,

O praise the Lord.

Slower.
Fine.
Allegro. ♩ = 96.

ly, is love - ly. Praise the Lord, ye house of
ly, is love - ly. Praise the Lord, ye house of
ly, is love - ly. Praise the Lord, ye house of
ly, is love - ly. Praise the Lord, ye house of

Is - ra - el; Praise the Lord, ye house of Aa - ron; Praise the Lord,
Is - ra - el; Praise the Lord, ye house of Aa - ron; Praise the Lord,
Is - ra - el; Praise the Lord, ye house of Aa - ron; Praise the Lord,
Is - ra - el; Praise the Lord, ye house of Aa - ron; Praise the Lord,

D. C.

ye house of Le - vi; Ye that fear the Lord, praise the Lord, praise the Lord.
ye house of Le - vi; Ye that fear the Lord, praise the Lord, praise the Lord.
ye house of Le - vi; Ye that fear the Lord, praise the Lord, praise the Lord.
ye house of Le - vi; Ye that fear the Lord, praise the Lord, praise the Lord.

I will alway give Thanks.

I will alway give Thanks.

I will alway give Thanks.

mouth, My soul shall make her boast, her boast in the Lord, the hum-ble shall
mouth, My soul shall make her boast, her boast in the Lord, the hum-ble shall
mouth, My soul shall make her boast, her boast in the Lord, the hum-ble shall
mouth, My soul shall make her boast, her boast in the Lord, the hum-ble shall
hear there-of and... be glad. O praise the Lord with
hear there-of and... be glad. O praise the Lord, O praise the Lord with
hear there-of and... be glad. O praise the Lord, O praise the Lord with
hear there-of and... be glad. O praise the Lord, O praise the Lord with
me, and let.... us mag-ni-fy His Name to-geth-er. A - men....
me, and let us mag-ni-fy His Name to-geth-er. A - men....
me,... and let... us mag-ni-fy His Name to-geth-er. A - men....
me,... and let.... us mag-ni-fy His Name to-geth-er. A - men....

Blessed are they that dwell in Thy house.

strength is in Thee; In whose heart are Thy ways, In whose heart are Thy ways,
strength is in Thee; In whose heart are Thy ways,.. who,
is in Thee; In whose heart are Thy ways, in whose heart are Thy ways,
strength is in Thee; In whose heart are Thy ways,.. who,
use it for a well,
go-ing thro' the vale of mis-e-ry, use it for a well,.... who,
use it for a well,
go-ing thro' the vale of mis-e-ry, use it for a well,.... who,
use it for a well; and the
go-ing thro' the vale of mis-e-ry, use it for a well; and the
use it for a well; and the
go-ing thro' the vale of mis-e-ry, use it for a well;

Blessed are they that dwell in Thy House.

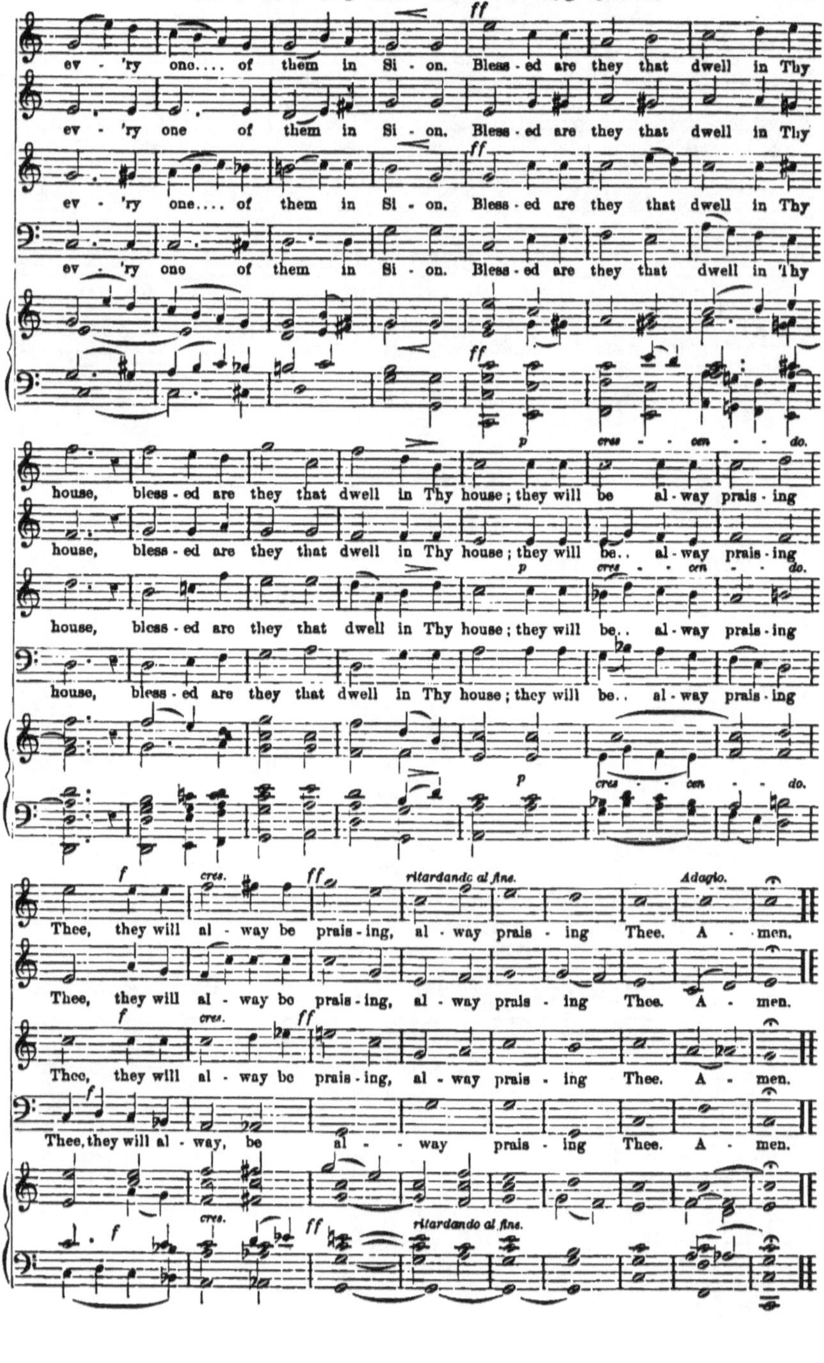
ff
ev - 'ry one.... of them in Si - on. Bless - ed are they that dwell in Thy
ev - 'ry one of them in Si - on. Bless - ed are they that dwell in Thy
ff
ev - 'ry one.... of them in Si - on. Bless - ed are they that dwell in Thy
ev - 'ry one of them in Si - on. Bless - ed are they that dwell in Thy
ff
p cres - - cen - - do.
house, bless - ed are they that dwell in Thy house; they will be al - way prais - ing
house, bless - ed are they that dwell in Thy house; they will be.. al - way prais - ing
p cres - - cen - - do.
house, bless - ed are they that dwell in Thy house; they will be.. al - way prais - ing
house, bless - ed are they that dwell in Thy house; they will be.. al - way prais - ing
p cres - - cen - - do.
f cres. ff ritardando al fine. Adagio.
Thee, they will al - way be prais - ing, al - way prais - ing Thee. A - men.
Thee, they will al - way be prais - ing, al - way prais - ing Thee. A - men.
f cres. ff
Thee, they will al - way be prais - ing, al - way prais - ing Thee. A - men.
f
Thee, they will al - way, be al - - way prais - ing Thee. A - men.
f cres. ff ritardando al fine.

In sweet Consent.

Join, ye bright planets, as ye shine, a loud Al-le-lu-ia; Join too, ye thunder, lightning, wind and
Join, ye bright planets, as ye shine, a loud Al-le-lu-ia; Join too, ye thunder, lightning, wind and
Join, ye bright planets, as ye shine, a loud Al-le-lu-ia; Join too, ye thunder, lightning, wind and
Join, ye bright planets, as ye shine, a loud Al-le-lu-ia; Join too, ye thunder, lightning, wind and
cloud, Al-le-lu-ia. Sing, groves and forests, flood, wave, storm and snow, Al-le-
cloud, Al-le-lu-ia. Sing, groves and forests, flood, wave, storm and snow, Al-le-
cloud, Al-le-lu-ia. Sing, groves and forests, flood, wave, storm and snow, Al-le-
cloud, Al-le-lu-ia. Sing, groves and forests, flood, wave, storm and snow, Al-le-
lu-ia; Answer, bright days, hoar frost, and sum-mer glow, Al-le-lu-ia.
lu-ia; Answer, bright days, hoar frost, and sum-mer glow, Al-le-lu-ia.
lu-ia; Answer, bright days, hoar frost, and sum-mer glow, Al-le-lu-ia.
lu-ia; Answer, bright days, hoar frost, and sum-mer glow, Al-le-lu-ia.
senza Ped.   Ped.

In sweet Consent.

Thou jubilant abyss of o-cean, cry Al-le-lu-ia; Ye tracts of earth and conti-nents, re-
Thou jubilant abyss of o-cean, cry Al-le-lu-ia; Ye tracts of earth and conti-nents, re-
Thou jubilant abyss of o-cean, cry Al-le-lu-ia; Ye tracts of earth and conti-nents, re-
Thou jubilant abyss of o-cean, cry Al-le-lu-ia; Ye tracts of earth and conti-nents, re-
ply, Al-le-lu-ia. Let the whole race of man the strain up-raise, Al-le-
ply, Al-le-lu-ia. Let the whole race of man the strain up-raise, Al-le-
ply, Al-le-lu-ia. Let the whole race of man the strain up-raise, Al-le-
ply, Al-le-lu-ia. Let the whole race of man the strain up-raise, Al-le-
lu-ia; And hymn their Maker in loud bursts of praise Al-le-lu-ia.
lu-ia; And hymn their Maker in loud bursts of praise: Al-le-lu-ia.
lu-ia; And hymn their Maker in loud bursts of praise: Al-le-lu-ia.
lu-ia; And hymn their Maker in loud bursts of praise: Al-le-lu-ia.

In sweet Consent.

With one glad shout from all be now outpoured Al - le - lu - ia; To Father, Son, and Spirit, God and
With one glad shout from all be now outpoured Al - le - lu - ia; To Father, Son, and Spirit, God and
With one glad shout from all be now outpoured Al - le - lu - ia; To Father, Son, and Spirit, God and
With one glad shout from all be now outpoured Al - le - lu - ia; To Father, Son, and Spirit, God and
Lord, Al - le - lu - ia. All glory, praise and worship be to Thee, Al - le -
Lord, Al - le - lu - ia. All glory, praise and worship be to Thee, Al - le -
Lord, Al - le - lu - ia. All glory, praise and worship be to Thee, Al - le -
Lord, Al - le - lu - ia. All glory, praise and worship be to Thee, Al - le -
lu - ia, Lord God Omnipotent, Blest Trin - i - ty, Al - le - lu - ia. A - - men.
lu - ia, Lord God Omnipotent, Blest Trin - i - ty, Al - le - lu - ia. A - - men.
lu - ia, Lord God Omnipotent, Blest Trin - i - ty, Al - le - lu - ia. A - - men.
lu - ia, Lord God Omnipotent, Blest Trin - i - ty, Al - le - lu - ia. A - - men.

O give Thanks unto the Lord.

Psalm cv. 1, 2. | Sir George Job Elvey, Mus. D. (1816 —).

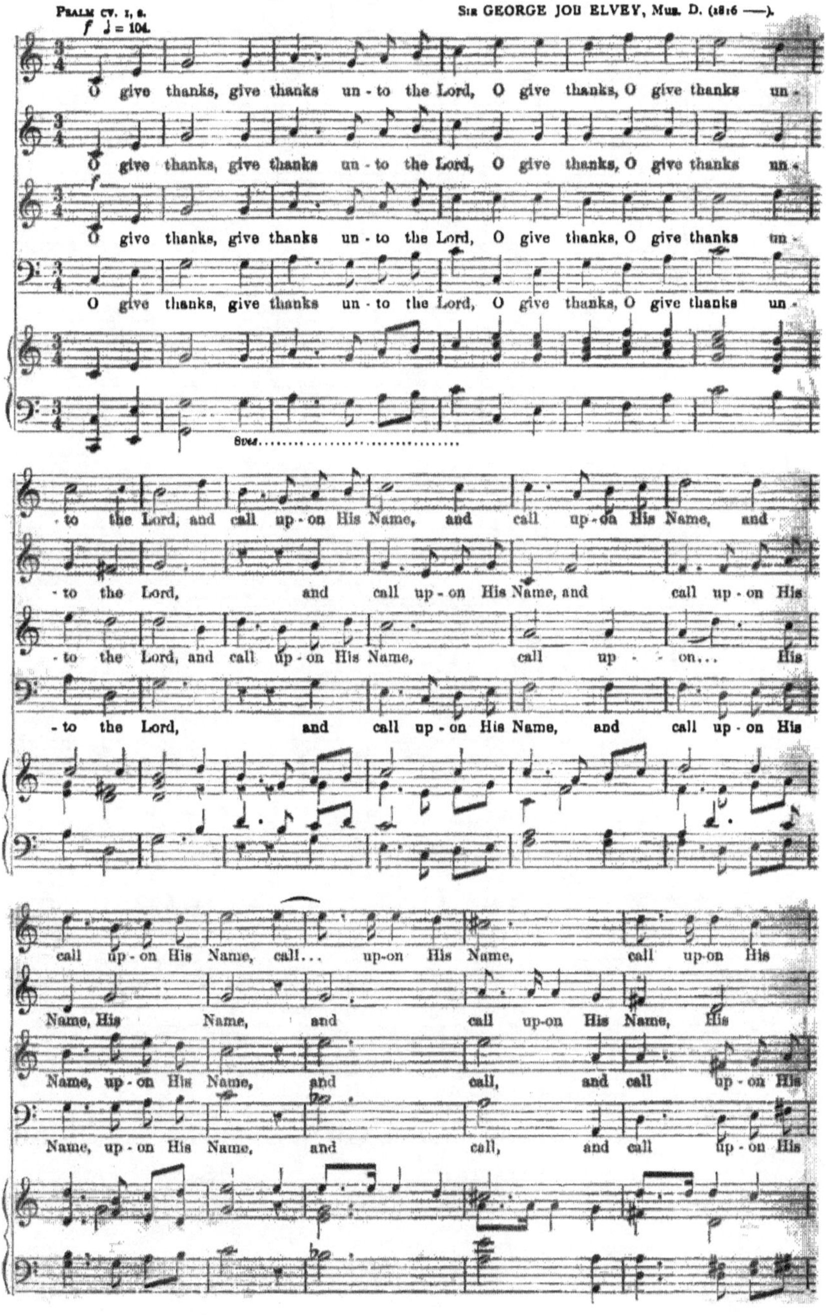

Name, and call up-on His Name, call.... up-on His Name.
Name, call... up-on His Name, His Name, up - on His Name.
Name, and call up-on His Name, call up - on His Name. Tell the
Name, and call up-on His Name, call up - on His Name.
Tell the peo - ple what things, tell the peo - ple what
Tell the peo - ple what things, tell the
peo - ple what things, what things He hath done, tell,
Tell the peo - ple what things, what things, tell the peo - ple what
things, tell the peo - ple what things He hath done; tell the peo - ple what
peo - ple what things, what things He hath done; tell the peo - ple what
tell the peo - ple what things He hath done; tell the peo - ple what
things, tell the peo - ple what things He hath done; tell the peo - ple what

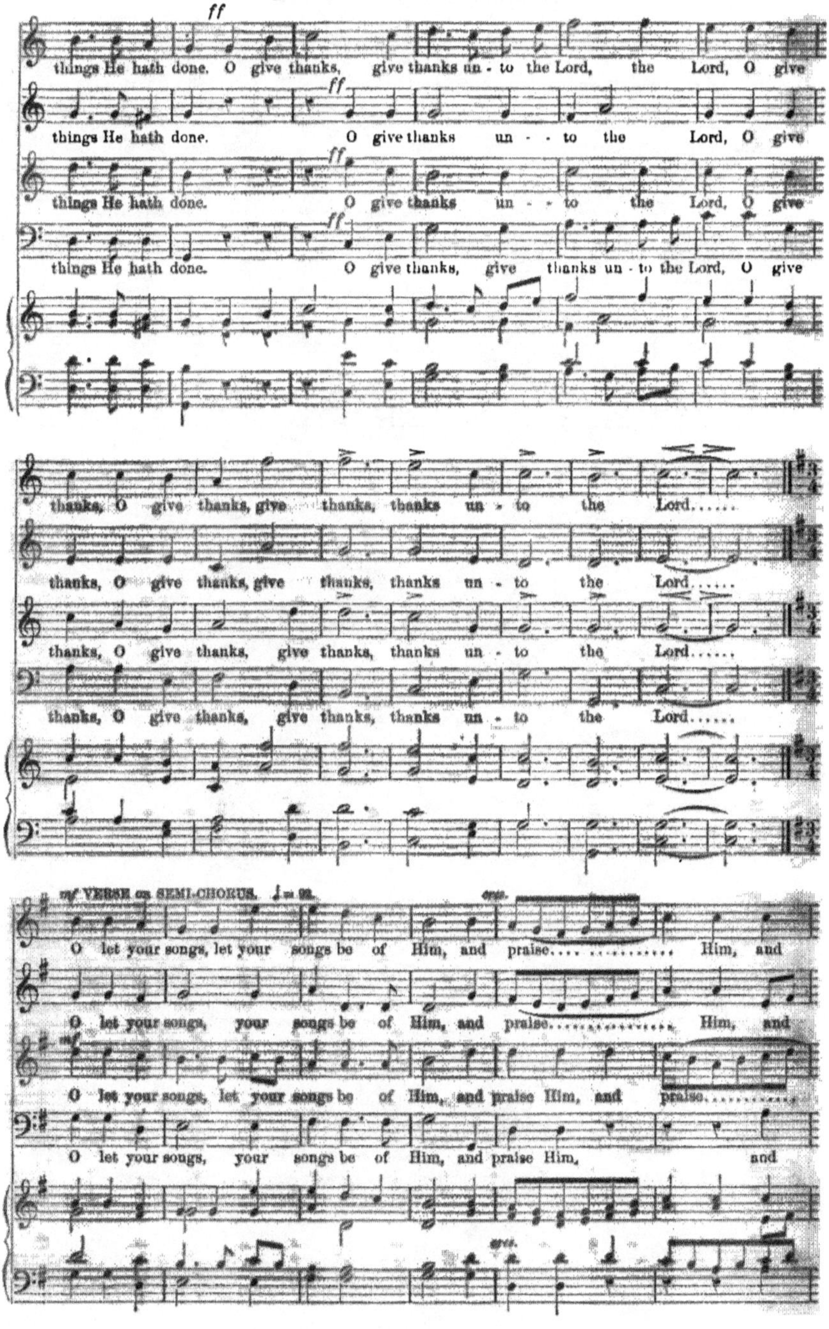

O give Thanks unto the Lord.

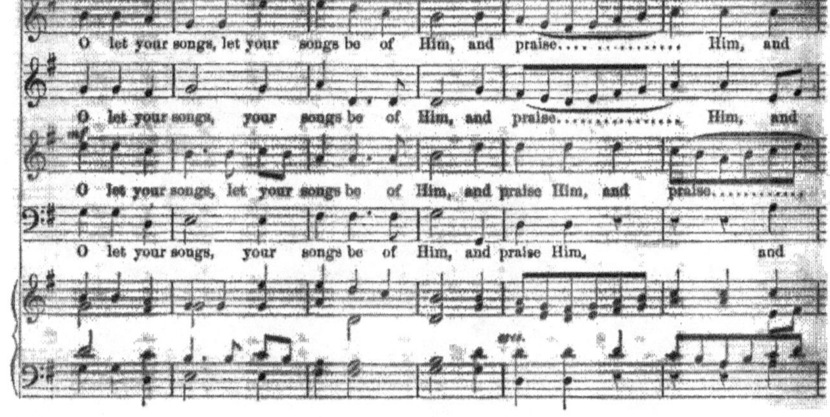

praise Him, and praise Him. O let your songs be of Him, and praise..........
praise Him, and praise Him. O let your songs be of Him, and praise.......
.... Him, and praise Him. O..... let your songs be of Him, and praise Him,
praise................. Him, O let your songs be of... Him, and praise Him, and
.... Him, O....... let your songs be of Him, and praise Him, and praise Him, and
.... Him, O let your songs be of Him, and praise Him, and praise Him, and
O. .... let your songs be of Him, and praise Him, and praise Him, and
praise................. Him, your songs be of Him, and praise Him, and praise Him, and
let your talk-ing be of all His won-drous works, and let your
let your talk-ing be of all...... His won-drous works, let your
let your talk-ing be of all...... His won--drous works, let your
let your talk-ing be of all His won-drous works, let your
cres.
cres.
ff
ff
ff
mf
mf
poco a poco dim.

O give Thanks unto the Lord.

that seek the Lord, that seek the Lord, Let the heart of them re-
Let the heart of them re - joice, re - joice, Let the heart of
joice, re - joice, that seek the Lord, Let the
that seek the Lord, that seek the Lord, Let..... the
- joice that seek the Lord, Let the heart............ of them re - joice that seek the
them re - joice, the heart of them re - joice, of them re - joice that seek the
heart of them re - joice, Let the heart of them re - joice that seek the
heart of them re - joice, Let the heart of them re - joice, Let the heart of them rejoice that seek the
Lord, Let the heart of them re - joice that seek, that seek the Lord. A - men.
Lord, re - - joice............ that seek, that.. seek... the Lord. A - men.
Lord, Let the heart of them re - joice that seek,.. that seek... the Lord. A - men.
Lord, Let the heart of them re - joice that seek,.. that seek the Lord. A - men.
14

O taste and see how gracious the Lord is.

PSALM XXXIV. 8—10.

SIR JOHN GOSS, MUS. D. (1800—1880).

VERSE.—*Andante e con espressione.* ♩ = 112.

FULL. m
bless - ed is the man that trust - eth in Him. O taste and see how
bless - ed is the man that trust - eth in Him. O taste and see how
bless - ed is the man that trust - eth in Him. O taste.......... how
bless - ed is the man that trust - eth in Him. O taste and see how
gra - cious the Lord is, bless - ed is the man that trust - eth in Him.
gra - cious the Lord is, bless - ed is the man that trust - eth in Him. O
gra - cious the Lord is, bless - ed is the man that trust - eth in Him.
gra - cious the Lord is, bless - ed is the man that trust - eth in Him.
O taste and see,.......... taste and see, taste and see how
taste and see, and see, taste,........ taste and see how
O taste and see, taste and see, taste........ and see how
O taste and see, taste and see, and see how

O taste and see how gracious the Lord is.

But they who seek the Lord, they who seek the
But they who seek the Lord, who seek the
But they who seek the Lord, they who seek the
hun - ger, But they who seek the Lord, they who seek the
Lord.............. shall want no man - ner of thing that is good, shall want no
Lord.............. shall want no man - ner of thing.... that is good,.
Lord.............. shall want no thing that is good, no
Lord, who seek the Lord, shall want no thing............. that is good,......
man - ner of thing that is good, shall want no man - ner of thing that is good, no man - ner of
.... shall want,........ shall want no man - ner of thing that is good, no man - ner of
thing that is good, shall want no man - ner of thing that is good, no man - ner of
.... shall want,........ shall want no man - ner of thing that is good, no man - ner of

O taste and see how gracious the Lord is.

thing that is good. The li-ons do lack, and suf-fer hun - ger, and suf-fer
thing that is good. The li-ons do lack, and suf-fer
thing that is good. The li-ons do lack, and suf-fer
thing that is good. The li-ons do lack, and suf-fer
hun - ger, but they who seek the Lord, they who seek the
hun - ger, but they who seek the Lord, who seek the
hun - ger, but they who seek the Lord, they who seek the
hun - ger, but they who seek the Lord, they who seek the
Lord.................. shall want no man - ner of thing that is good, shall want no
Lord.................. shall want no man - ner of thing.......... that is good,....
Lord.................. shall want no thing that is good, no
Lord, who seek the Lord shall want no thing............ that is good,......

man - ner of thing that is good, shall want no man - ner of thing that is good, no man-ner of
.... shall want,....... shall want no man - ner of thing that is good, no man - ner of
thing that is good, shall want no man - ner of thing that is good, no man - ner of
.... shall want,....... shall want no man - ner of thing that is good, no man-ner of
thing that is good. O taste and see how gra - cious the
thing that is good. O taste and see how gra - cious the
thing that is good. O taste and see how gra - cious the
thing that is good. O taste and see how gra - cious the
Lord is, bless - ed is the man...... that trust - eth in Him.
Lord is, bless - ed is the man...... that trust - eth in Him.
Lord is, bless - ed is the man...... that trust - eth in Him.
Lord is, bless - ed is the man...... that trust - eth in Him.
p Slower.
p Slower.

Behold now, praise ye the Lord.

PSALM CXXXIV. I.

JOHN BAPTISTE CALKIN (1827 ——).

Andante maestoso.   ♩ = 122.

mf

Ped.

SOLO.*—Bass.

CHORUS.

Ped.

* This Solo may be given to all the Bass Voices.

night stand............ in the house of the Lord.
night stand............ in the house of the Lord.
Lord; Ye that by night stand in the house of the Lord. E - ven in the
SOLO.
night stand in the house of the Lord.
mp
Man.
SOLO.
in... the house............ of the
house, the house of the Lord our God, in... the house of the
SOLI.
in... the house, the house of the
mf SOLO.
E - ven in the house, the house of the Lord our
Lord our God, E - ven in the house of
mf
Lord our.. God, E - - ven in........ the house........ of
1st Bass.
Lord..... our God, E - ven in the house of
mf

Behold now, praise ye the Lord.

SOLO.
in.... the house........... of the Lord our
house of the Lord our God, in.... the house of the Lord..... our
SOLO.
in.... the house........... of the Lord our..
SOLO.
in.... the house, the house of the Lord our
God, the house of the Lord our
God,
God, the house, in the house......... of God,
God, e - ven in the house, the house of the Lord our God, in the
God, the house of God, e - ven the house of God,
the house of God,
the house of God,.. the house of God, the house of
house, the house of God, the house of God, in the house, the

Behold now, praise ye the Lord.

praise ye the Lord, ye serv-ants of......... the Lord,
Lord, praise the Lord, ye serv-ants of......... the Lord,
Lord, praise the Lord, ye serv-ants of......... the Lord, now,
Lord, praise the Lord, Be-hold now, praise ye the
Lord, praise the Lord, ye serv-ants of............... the Lord, praise the
now, praise ye the Lord, ye serv-ants of...... the
now, praise ye the Lord, praise the Lord, ye serv-ants of...... the
praise ye the Lord... praise the Lord, praise the Lord, ye serv-ants of...... the
Lord, ye serv-ants of the Lord, praise the Lord, ye serv-ants of...... the
Lord, now, praise the Lord, now, praise the Lord, praise the Lord.
Lord, now, praise the Lord, now, praise the Lord, praise the Lord.
Lord, now, praise the Lord, now, praise the Lord, praise the Lord.
Lord, now, praise the Lord, now, praise the Lord, praise the Lord.

O praise the Lord.

God. O praise the Lord, laud ye the name of the Lord, praise it, O ye
God..... O praise the Lord, laud ye the name of the Lord,........ praise it, O ye
God..... O praise the Lord, laud ye.... the name of the Lord, praise it, O ye
God...... O praise the Lord, laud ye the name of the Lord,......... praise it, O ye
serv - ants of the Lord.
serv - ants of the Lord.
serv - ants of the Lord.
serv - ants of the Lord.
p Piu animato.
O praise..... the Lord,........ for the Lord........ is gra -

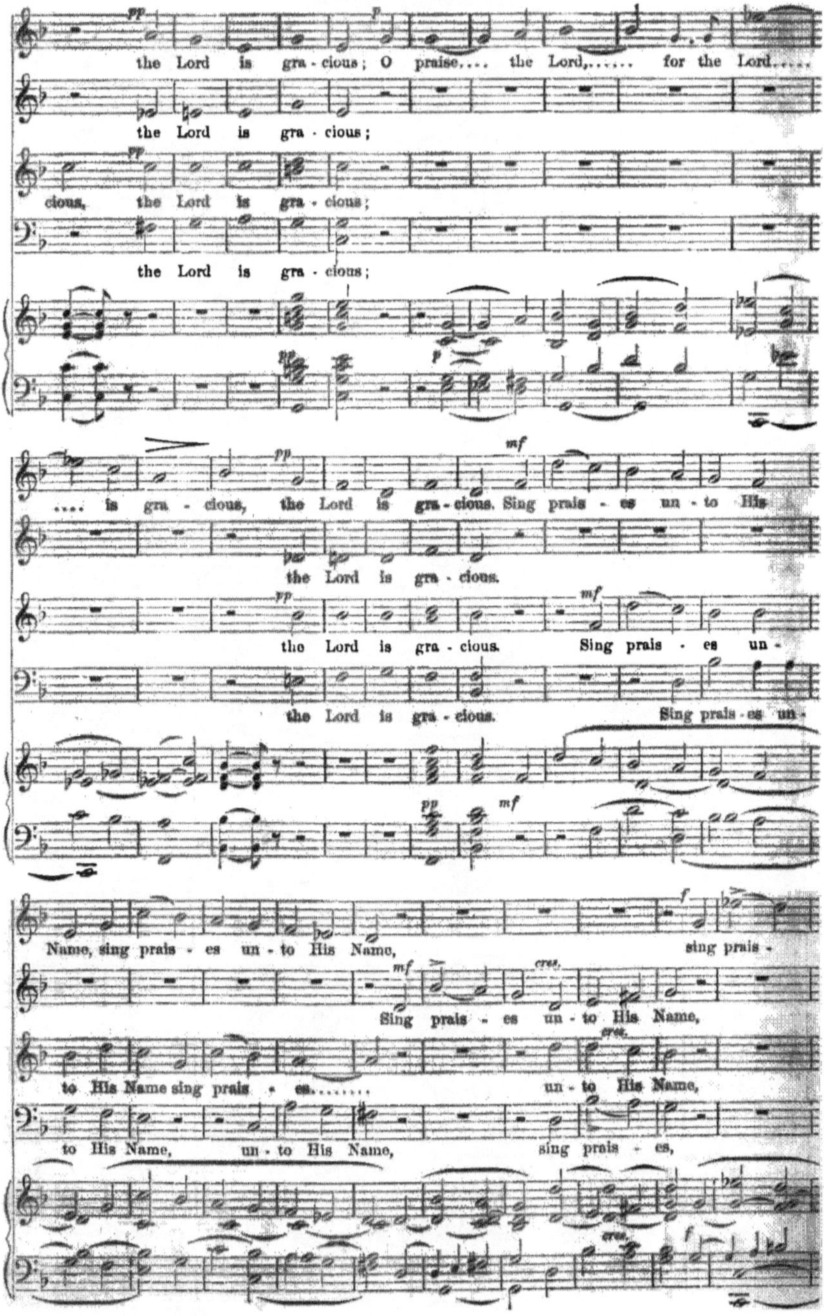
pp
the Lord is gra - cious; O praise.... the Lord,...... for the Lord.....
the Lord is gra - cious;
cious, the Lord is gra - cious;
the Lord is gra - cious;
.... is gra - cious, the Lord is gra - cious. Sing prais - es un - to His
the Lord is gra - cious.
the Lord is gra - cious. Sing prais - es un -
the Lord is gra - cious. Sing prais - es un -
mf
Name, sing prais - es un - to His Name, sing prais -
Sing prais - es un - to His Name,
to His Name sing prais - es........ un - to His Name,
to His Name, un - to His Name, sing prais - es,
cres.

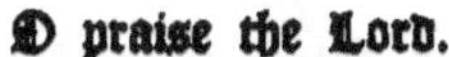

O praise the Lord.

ff
- es un - to His Name, sing prais - es, sing prais - es un - to His Name;
un - to His Name, sing prais - es, sing prais - es un - to His Name;
sing prais - es, sing prais - es, sing prais - es un - to His Name;
sing prais - es un - to His Name;

Tranquillo. p
for it is love - - - ly, for it is love - - -
pp
for it is love - - -
for it is love - - - -
for it is love - -

dim - in - u - en - do. p
ly For why? For why?
ly For why? For why?
ly dim in - u - en do. For why? For why? mf più lento.
ly For why? For why? Thy
più lento

O praise the Lord.

Lord is great, our Lord... is great, and that our Lord is a-bove all gods,
Lord is great, our Lord... is great, and that our Lord is a-bove all gods,
Lord is great, our Lord is great, and that our Lord is a-bove all gods,
.... and that our Lord is great, and that our Lord is a-bove all gods,
is a-bove all gods, that our Lord is a-bove all gods, that our
is a-bove...... all gods, that our Lord is a-bove all gods, that our
is a-bove.. all gods, that our Lord is a-bove all gods, that our
is a-bove.. all gods, that our Lord is a-bove all... gods, that our
Lord is a-bove.............. all gods................. A - men.
Lord is a-bove............ all gods.................. A - men.
Lord is a-bove.................. all gods.............. A - men.
Lord is a-bove................ all gods................. A - men.

Praise God in His Holiness.

mf
praise Him in the fir - - mament, in the fir - - mament of His pow - er,
praise Him in the fir - mament, in the fir - - mament of His pow - er,
mf
praise Him in the fir - mament, in the fir - - mament of His pow - er,
praise Him in the fir - ma - ment.......... of His pow - er,
mf
praise Him in the fir - - mament, in the fir - mament of His pow - er,
praise Him in the fir - - mament, in the fir - mament of His pow - er,
praise Him in the fir - - mament, in the fir - mament of His pow - er,
praise Him in the fir - ma - ment.......... of His pow - er,
f cres - cen - do. ff
praise Him, praise Him, praise Him, praise Him, praise God in His ho - li - ness, praise
praise Him, praise Him, praise Him, praise Him, praise God in His ho - li - ness, praise
f cres - cen - do. ff
praise Him, praise Him, praise Him, praise Him, praise God in His ho - li - ness, praise
praise Him, praise Him, praise Him, praise Him, praise God in His ho - li - ness, praise
f cres - cen - do. ff

Praise God in His Holiness.

chil-dren, praise.. the Name,.. the Name of the Lord, Young men and maid-ens,
chil-dren, praise.. the Name,.. the Name of the Lord,.... Young men and maid-ens,
chil-dren, praise.. the Name,.. the Name of the Lord,...... Young men and maid-ens,
chil-dren, praise.. the Name,.. the Name of the Lord,........ Young men and maid-ens,
poco cres-cen-do. mf diminuendo.
old men and chil-dren, praise the Name,... the Name of the Lord,....
old men and chil-dren,.. praise................. the Name of the Lord,....
poco cres-cen-do mf diminuendo.
old men and chil-dren,.. praise the Name,... the Name of the Lord,....
old men and chil'-dren,.. praise................. the Name of the Lord,....
poco cres. mf dim. pp
pp
Young men and maid-ens,.. praise the Name of the Lord,..
pp
old men and chil-dren,. praise.... the Lord,
pp
Young men and maid-ens,.. praise the Name of the Lord,. the
.... old men.. and chil-dren,.. praise.... the Lord,...

Praise God in His Holiness.

praise..... the Lord,..
Praise the Name of the Lord,
praise..... the Lord,..
Praise the Name of the Lord,
Name of the Lord,..
Praise the Name of the Lord,
Praise the Name of the Lord,

pp poco a poco rallentando.
dim.
Praise.. the Name.. of..... the Lord...........
Praise.. the Name.. of..... the Lord...........
Praise.. the Name.. of..... the Lord...........
Praise.. the Name.. of..... the Lord...........
pp poco a poco. rall.
dim.
ppp

Maestoso. = 100.
ff
with glo - - ry,
with glo - - ry,
f ff f
Let the saints be joy-ful with glo - - ry, let the saints be
Let the saints be joy-ful with glo - - ry, let the saints be
f ff f

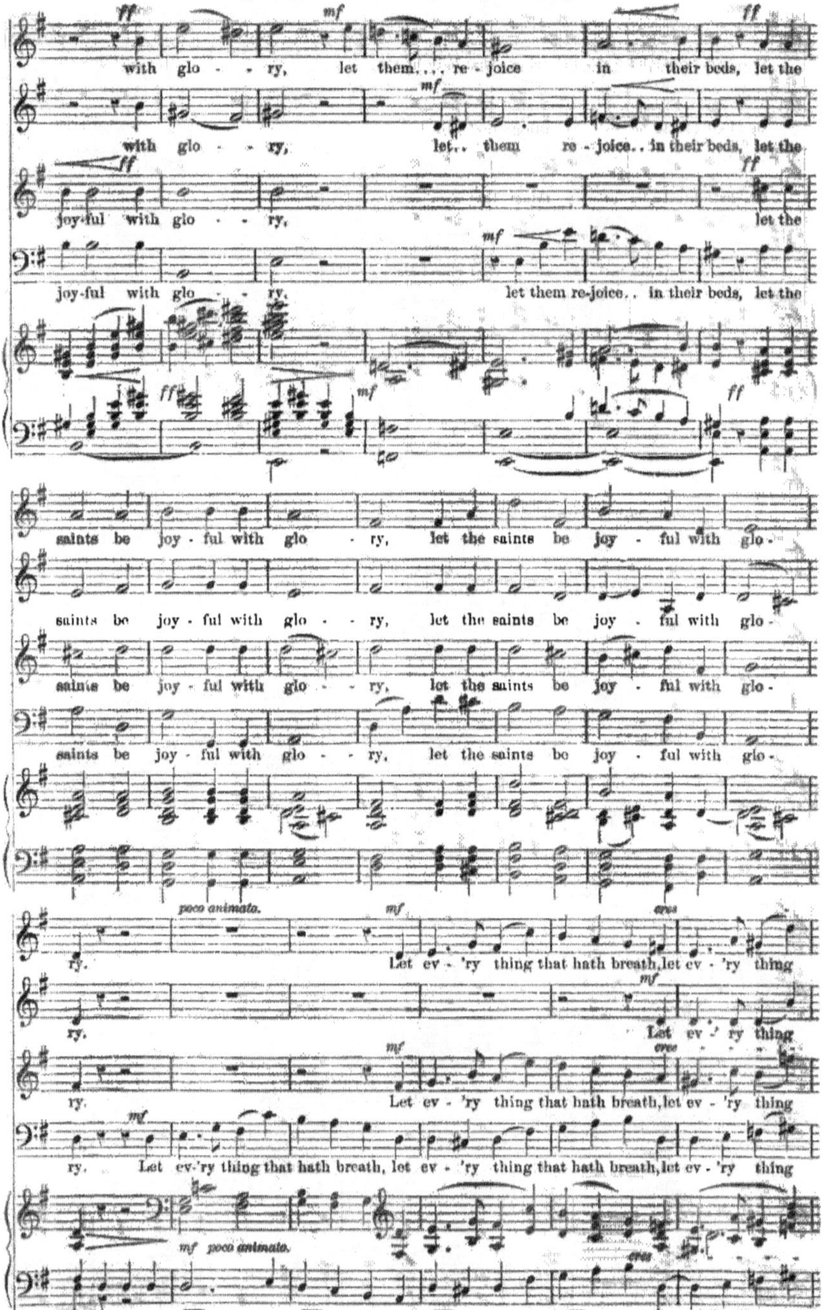
ff
with glo - - ry, let them... re - joice in their beds, let the
mf
with glo - - ry, let.. them re - joice.. in their beds, let the
ff
joy-ful with glo - - ry, let the
mf
joy-ful with glo - - ry, let them re-joice.. in their beds, let the
saints be joy - ful with glo - ry, let the saints be joy - ful with glo -
saints be joy - ful with glo - - ry, let the saints be joy - ful with glo -
saints be joy - ful with glo - - ry, let the saints be joy - ful with glo -
saints be joy - ful with glo - - ry, let the saints be joy - ful with glo -
poco animato.
cres
ry. Let ev - 'ry thing that hath breath, let ev - 'ry thing
ry. Let ev - 'ry thing
ry. Let ev - 'ry thing that hath breath, let ev - 'ry thing
ry. Let ev-'ry thing that hath breath, let ev - 'ry thing that hath breath, let ev - 'ry thing
mf poco animato.

Praise God in His Holiness.

tempo 1mo.
praise the Lord. Praise God, praise God,
praise the.. Lord. Praise God, praise
praise the Lord. Praise God, praise God,
praise the Lord. Praise God, praise
tempo 1mo.
Slower. ff
.... praise God, in His ho-li-ness, praise God, in His
God, praise God in His ho-li-ness, praise God, in His
.... praise God, in His ho-li-ness, praise God, in His
God, praise God in His ho-li-ness, praise God, in His
Slower. ff
ri - tar - dan - do.
ho-li-ness. A-men, A-men
ho-li-ness. A-men, A-men
ri - tar - dan - do.
ho-li-ness. A-men, A-men
ho-li-ness. A-men, A-men
ri - tar - dan - do.

O Lord, our Governor.

PSALM VIII. 1, 4, 5.

HENRY GADSBY (1842 ——).

Heav'ns!......
Lord, what is
Heav'ns!.....
Lord, what is
Heav'ns!......
Lord, what is
Heav'ns!......
Lord, what is
man.......... that Thou art mind - ful of him?...........
man.......... that Thou art mind - ful of him?...........
man.......... that Thou art mind - ful of him?...........
man that Thou art mind - ful of him?...........
Lord, what is man......... that Thou art mind - ful
Lord, what is man......... that Thou art mind - ful
Lord, what is man......... that Thou art mind - ful
Lord, what is man......... that Thou art mind - ful
ff mf dim. p
ff p

of him? Or the son of man....... that Thou vis-
of him? Or the son.. of... man.... that Thou....... vis-
of him? Or the son of man....... that Thou vis-
of him? Or the son of man....... that Thou vis-
it - est him?...... Thou mad - est him low - er than the
it - est him?...... Thou mad - est him low - er than the
it - est him?...... Thou mad - est him low - er than the
it - est him?...... Thou mad - est him low - er than the
An - - gels;..... Thou mad - est him low - er than the
An - - gels;..... Thou mad - est him low - er than the
An - - gels;..... Thou mad - est him low - er than the
An - - gels;..... Thou mad - est him low - er than the
cres.
dim.
Sotto voce.
Sotto voce.
cres.
dim.

An - gels;..... To crown.. him, to crown.. him with
An - gels;..... To crown... him, to crown,. him with
An - gels;..... To crown... him, to crown.. him with
An - gels;..... To crown... him, to crown.. him with
glo - ry! To crown him, to crown him with glo - ry, with
glo - ry! To crown him, to crown him with glo - ry, with
glo - ry! To crown him, to crown him with glo - ry, with
glo - ry! To crown him, to crown him with glo - ry, with
glo - ry and wor - ship, to..... crown him.... with glo-
glo - ry and wor - ship, to crown....... him with
glo - ry and wor - ship, to crown him,.... to
glo - ry and wor - ship, to crown him with glo-

- ry, glo - ry and wor - - ship, to crown him with
glo - - ry,..... glo - ry and wor - - ship, to crown him with
crown him...... with glo - ry and wor - - ship, to crown him with
- ry, with glo - ry and wor - - ship, to crown him with
glo - ry and wor - - ship. O Lord, our Gov - ern - or, how
glo - ry and wor - - ship. O Lord, our Gov - ern - or, how
glo - ry and wor - - ship. O Lord, our Gov - ern - or, how
glo - ry and wor - ship. O Lord, our Gov - ern - or, how
ex - cel - lent Thy Name! how ex - cel - lent Thy
ex - cel - lent Thy Name! how ex - - cel -
ex - cel - lent Thy Name! how ex - - cel -
ex - cel - lent Thy Name! how ex - cel - lent Thy

Name in all, in all the world! Thou that hast set Thy.. Glo -
lent Thy Name in all the world! Thou that hast set Thy.. Glo -
lent Thy Name in all the world! Thou that hast set Thy.. Glo -
Name in all, in all the world! Thou that hast set Thy.. Glo -
ry a - bove.... .... the Heav'ns, how ex - - cel - lent Thy
ry a - bove the Heav'ns....... how ex - cel - - lent Thy
ry a - bove the Heav'ns...... how ex - cel - - lent Thy
ry a - bove the Heav'ns,...... how ex - cel - - lent Thy
Name, O Lord, Thy Name, O Lord, how ex - cel - lent in all the
Name, O Lord, Thy Name, O Lord, how ex - cel - lent in all........... the
Name, O Lord, Thy Name, O Lord, how ex - cel - lent in all the
Name, O Lord, Thy Name, O Lord, how ex - cel - lent in all the

world......... how ex - - cel - lent! how ex - - cel - lent! how ex - cel -
world......... how ex - - cel - lent! how ex - - cel - lent! how ex - cel -
world......... how ex - - cel - lent! how ex - - cel - lent! how ex - cel -
world......... how ex - - cel - lent! how ex - - cel - lent! how ex - cel -
lent Thy Name,........ how ex - cel - lent Thy Name,......... O Lord,
lent Thy Name, O Lord, how ex - cel - lent Thy Name, O Lord, O Lord,
lent Thy Name, O Lord, how ex - cel - lent Thy Name, O Lord, O Lord,
lent Thy Name,.... .... how ex - cel - lent Thy Name,........ O Lord,
our Gov - ern - or, how ex - cel - lent Thy Name in all, in all.... the world.
our Gov - ern - or, how ex - cel - lent Thy Name in all, in all....... the world.
our Gov - ern - or, how ex - cel - lent Thy Name in all, in all.... the world.
our Gov - ern - or, how ex - cel - lent Thy Name in all, in all.... the world.
rall.
rall.
rall.

Psalms CXIII. 2, 5; CIV. 13, 14.

HENRY GADSBY (1842 ——).

Allegro. ♩ = 120.

Blessed be the Name of the Lord.

are in heav-en and earth? Who is like un-to the Lord our God, that
are in heav-en and earth? Who is like un-to the Lord our God, that
are in heav-en and earth? Who is like un-to the Lord our God, that
are in heav-en and earth? Who is like un-to the Lord our God, that
hath His dwell-ing so high, and yet hum-bleth Himself to be-hold the things that
hath His dwell-ing so high, and yet hum-bleth Himself to be-hold the things that
hath His dwell-ing so high, and yet hum-bleth Himself to be-hold the things that
hath His dwell-ing so high, and yet hum-bleth Himself to be-hold the things that
are in heav-en and earth? He wa-ter-eth the hills from a-bove,
are in earth? He wa-ter-eth the hills from a-bove, He
are in earth?
are in earth? He

Blessed be the Name of the Lord.

The earth is fill'd with the fruit of Thy works, is
wa-ter-eth the hills from a-bove. The earth is fill'd with the fruit of Thy works, is
wa-ter-eth the hills from a-bove.
fill'd with the fruit of Thy works.
fill'd with the fruit of Thy works.
He bring-eth forth grass for the cat-tle, and green
He bring-eth forth grass for the cat-tle, and green
He bring-eth forth grass for the cat-tle, and green
He bring--eth forth grass, and green
herb for the serv-ice of men, He bring-eth forth grass for the cat-tle,
herb for the serv-ice of men, He bring--eth forth grass,

herb for the serv-ice of men,........ and green herb for the serv-ice of men.
herb for the serv-ice of men, and green herb for the serv-ice of men,
green herb for the serv-ice of men, green herb for the serv-ice of
green herb for the serv-ice of men, green herb for the serv-ice of
Bless - ed, bless - ed, bless - ed, bless - ed, bless - ed be the
Bless - ed, bless - ed, bless - ed, bless - ed, bless - ed be the
men........ Bless - ed, bless - ed, bless - ed, bless - ed be the
men........ Bless - ed, bless - ed, bless - ed, bless - ed be the
Name of the Lord from this time forth and for ev - er-more, bless - ed be the
Name of the Lord from this time forth and for ev - er-more, bless - ed be the
Name of the Lord from this time forth and for ev - er-more, bless - ed be the
Name of the Lord from this time forth and for ev - er-more, bless - ed be the

Blessed be the Name of the Lord.

bless - ed, bless - ed, bless - ed be the Name of the Lord, bless - ed,
bless - ed, bless - ed, bless - ed be the Name of the Lord, bless - ed,
bless - ed, bless - ed, bless - ed be the Name of the Lord, bless - ed,
bless - ed, bless - ed, bless - ed be the Name of the Lord, bless - ed,
bless - ed, bless - ed be the Name of the Lord from this time forth and for ev -
bless - ed, bless - ed be the Name of the Lord from this time forth and for ev -
bless - ed, bless - ed be the Name of the Lord from this time forth and for ev -
bless - ed, bless - ed be the Name of the Lord from this time forth and for ev -
rall.
rall.
ped. doppio.
er - more
er - more
er - more
- er - more

Sing Praises to God.

* The Organ accompaniment may be used in the places thus marked; but the effect is much better when performed as directed.

our God for-ev-er and ev-er, sing prais-es, prais-es un-
our God for-ev-er and ev-er, sing prais-es, prais-es
sing prais-es, prais-es
sing prais-es, prais-es
pp
pp
pp Organ.
to the Lord, sing prais-es... un-to God,
to the Lord, sing un-to God,
to the Lord, O sing prais-es... un-to God,
to the Lord,
mp
Ped.
sing prais-es un-to... God.
sing prais-es un-to God.
sing un-to... God.
O sing prais-es un-to God.
mp
molto rall.
p

Sing Praises to God.

molto rall.
a tempo.
fields are white to har - vest.
molto rall.
a tempo.
p
Allegro.
p
f   ff
Ped.
CHORUS.
mf
Sing praises un-to God, sing prais - - - - es, re-
mf
Sing praises un-to God, sing prais - - - - es, re-
mf
Sing praises un-to God, O sing prais - - - - es, re-
mf
Sing praises un-to God, O sing prais - - - - es, re-
mf

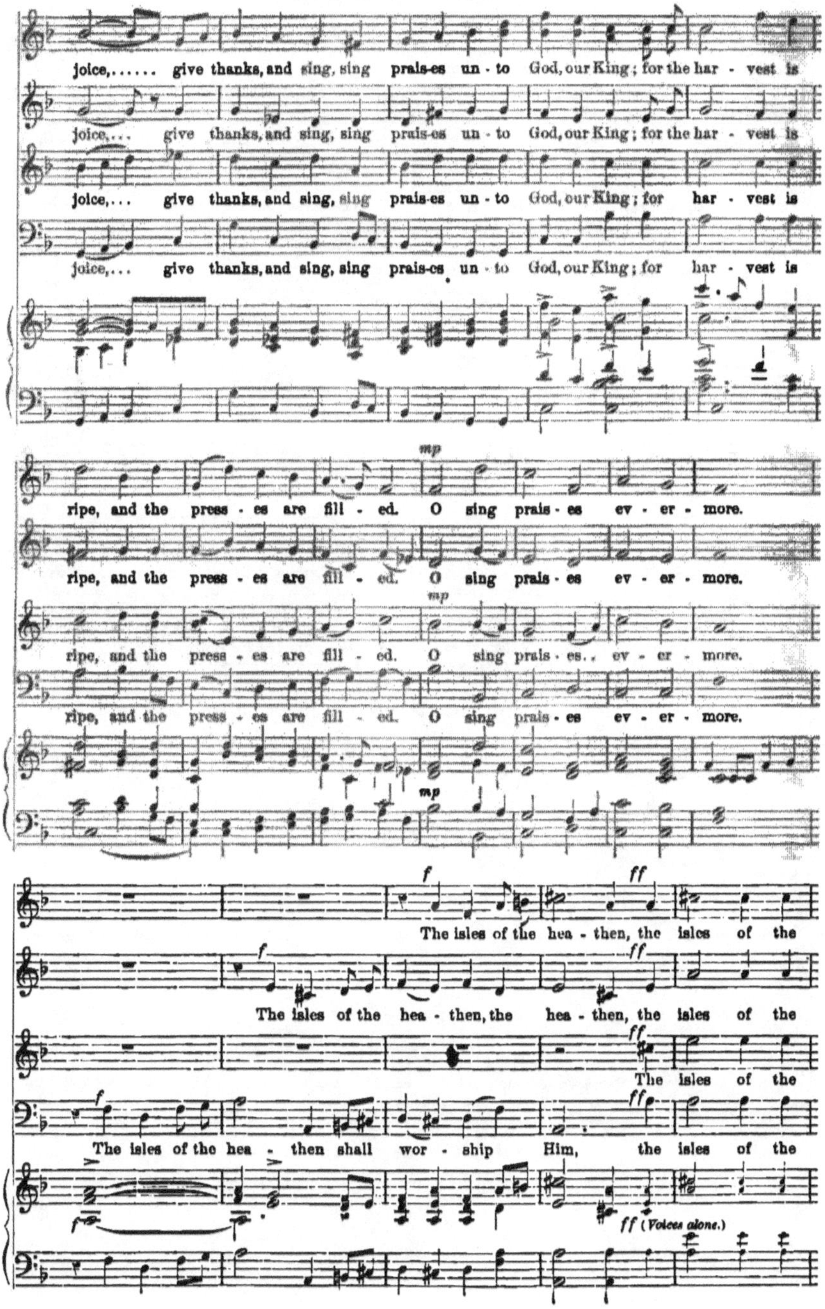
joice,...... give thanks, and sing, sing prais-es un - to God, our King; for the har - vest is
joice,... give thanks, and sing, sing prais-es un - to God, our King; for the har - vest is
joice,... give thanks, and sing, sing prais-es un - to God, our King; for har - vest is
joice,... give thanks, and sing, sing prais-es un - to God, our King; for har - vest is
mp
ripe, and the press - es are fill - ed. O sing prais - es ev - er - more.
ripe, and the press - es are fill - ed. O sing prais - es ev - er - more.
mp
ripe, and the press - es are fill - ed. O sing prais - es.. ev - er - more.
ripe, and the press - es are fill - ed. O sing prais - es ev - er - more.
mp
f
ff
The isles of the hea - then, the isles of the
f
ff
The isles of the hea - then, the hea - then, the isles of the
ff
The isles of the
f
ff
The isles of the hea - then shall wor - ship Him, the isles of the
ff (Voices alone.)

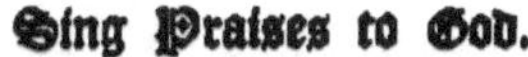

hea - then shall wor - ship Him.
hea - then shall wor - ship Him. The isles of the
hea - then shall wor - ship Him. The isles of the hea - then shall
hea - then shall wor - ship Him.
Organ.
Senza Ped. Ped.
f ff p dolce.
The isles of the hea - then, the isles of the hea - then shall wor - ship Him. For our
hea - then, the hea - then, the isles of the hea - then shall wor - ship Him. For our
ff
wor - ship Him, the isles of the hea - then shall wor - ship Him.
The isles of the hea - then shall wor - ship Him.
(Voices alone.)
p Organ.
God hath not for - sak - en us, for - sak - en us,........ but hath had mer - cy up-
God hath not for - sak - en us, for - sak - en us,........
p dolce.
For our God hath not for - sak - en us,.......... but hath had mer - cy up-
p dolce.
He hath not for - sak - en us.

Sing Praises to God.

prais - es to God, O ye king-doms of the earth,... O sing prais - es
prais - es to God, O ye king-doms of the earth,...... O sing prais - es
ev - - - er. Al - le - 'lu - - ia,
ev - - - er. Al - le - lu - - ia,
Al - le - lu - - ia,.....
Al - le - lu - - ia,
f Organ.
Al - le - lu - - ia.................
Al - le - lu - - ia.................
Al - le - lu - - ia.................
Al - le - lu - - ia.................
17

Now Autumn strews on every Plain.

Mrs. FELICIA DOROTHEA HEMANS (1793—1835).

ELIZABETH STIRLING (1819 —⟶

o'er the land, And to the God of na-ture raise The grateful song, the hymn of praise.
.... And to the God of na-ture raise The grateful song, the hymn of praise.
o'er the land, And to the God of na-ture raise The grateful song, the hymn of praise.
... And to the God of na-ture raise The grateful song, the hymn of praise.
The in-fant corn in ver-nal hours He nur-tur'd with His gen-tle show'rs, And bade the Summer
The in-fant corn in ver-nal hours He nur-tur'd with His gen-tle show'rs, And bade the Summer
The in-fant corn in ver-nal hours He nur-tur'd with His gen-tle show'rs, And bade the Summer
The in-fant corn in ver-nal hours He nur-tur'd with His gen-tle show'rs, And bade the Summer
clouds dif-fuse Their balm-y store of ge-nial dews. He mark'd the ten-der stem a-rise, Till
clouds dif-fuse Their balm-y store of ge-nial dews. He mark'd the ten-der stem a-rise, Till
clouds dif-fuse Their balm-y store of ge-nial dews. He mark'd the ten-der stem a-rise, Till
clouds dif-fuse Their balm-y store of ge-nial dews. He mark'd the ten-der stem a-rise, Till

Now Autumn strews on every Plain.

lay sin-cere, Whose boun-ty crowns the smil-ing year; The sounds from ev'ry woodland borne, The
lay sin-cere, Whose boun-ty crowns the smil-ing year; The sounds from ev'ry woodland borne, The
lay sin-cere, Whose boun-ty crowns the smil-ing year; The sounds from ev'ry woodland borne, The
lay sin-cere, Whose boun-ty crowns the smil-ing year; The sounds from ev'ry woodland borne, The
sighing winds that bend the corn, The yellow fields—around proclaim His might-y ev-er-
sighing winds that bend the corn, The fields................
sighing winds that bend the corn, The yellow fields—around proclaim His might-y ev-er-
sighing winds that bend the corn, The fields................
last-ing Name; To nature's God u-nit-ed raise The grateful song, the hymn of praise.
.... To nature's God u-nit-ed raise The grateful song, the hymn of praise.
last-ing Name; To nature's God u-nit-ed raise The grateful song, the hymn of praise.
.... To na-ture's God u-nit-ed raise The grateful song, the hymn of praise.

O Lord, how manifold are Thy Works.

JOSEPH BARNBY (1838 ——).

wis - dom hast Thou made them all. The earth is full, the earth is full of Thy
wis - dom hast Thou made them all. The earth is full,........ is full.. of Thy
wis - dom hast Thou made them all........ The earth is full, is full of Thy
made them all, in wis - dom hast Thou made them all. The earth is full of Thy
mf
rich - es. The val - leys stand so thick with corn that they laugh and sing, they laugh and
rich - es.
rich - es.
rich - es.
mf
sing, they laugh and sing, The val - leys stand so
they stand so
they laugh and sing, they laugh and sing, they stand so
they stand so

thick with corn, that they laugh and sing,   they laugh and sing...
thick with corn, that they laugh and sing.
thick with corn, that they laugh and sing,   they laugh and
thick with corn, that they laugh..... and sing, they laugh.. and sing.....
O Lord, how man - i - fold, how man - i - fold are Thy works :   in
O Lord, how man - i - fold, how man - i - fold are Thy works :   in
sing.   O Lord, how man - i - fold, how man - i - fold are Thy works :   in
O Lord, how man - i - fold, how man - i - fold are Thy works : in wis - dom,
wis - dom, in wis - dom hast Thou made.... them all.   O Lord, how
wis - dom, in wis - dom hast Thou made.... them all.   O Lord, how
wis - dom, in wis - dom hast Thou made.... them all.   O Lord, how
wis - - - dom hast Thou made.... them all.   O Lord, how

man - i-fold, how man-i-fold are Thy works; in wis - dom hast Thou made them all, in
man - i-fold, how man-i-fold are Thy works; in wis - dom hast Thou made them all, in
man - i-fold, how man-i-fold are Thy works, Thy works; in wis - dom hast Thou made them all, in
man - i-fold, how man-i-fold are Thy works; in wis - dom hast Thou
wis - dom hast Thou made them all, The earth is full, the earth is full of Thy
wis - dom hast Thou made them all, The earth is full,........ is full.. of Thy
wis - dom hast Thou made them all,........ The earth is full, is full of Thy
made them all, in wis - dom hast Thou made them all. The earth is full.. of Thy
rich - es. Praise the Lord, O my soul, Praise the Lord, O my
rich - es. Praise the Lord, O my soul, Praise the Lord, O my
rich - es. Praise the Lord, O my soul, Praise the Lord, O my
rich - es. Praise the Lord, O my soul, Praise the Lord, O my
ff

O Lord, how manifold are Thy Works.

Teach me, O Lord.

Teach me, O Lord.

stat - utes, shall keep it, shall keep it, and
stat - utes, shall keep it, shall keep it,
stat - utes, and I shall keep it, and I shall keep it,
stat - utes, shall keep it, shall keep it,
I shall keep it un - to... the.... end,.. shall keep it un-
shall keep it un - to the end, shall keep it un
shall keep it un - to the end,.. shall keep it un-
and I shall keep it un-
to...... the end, un - to...... the end.
to the end, un - to the end.
to the end, un - to the end.
to the end, un - to...... the end.

If ye love Me.

St. John xiv. 15, 16.

CHARLES SWINNERTON HEAP, Mus. D. (1847 —)

Andante moderato.

poco più animato.
Com - forter, that He may a - bide with you for - ev - er, with you for-
Com - forter, that He may a - bide with you for - ev - er,
Com - forter, that He may a - bide with you for-
Com - forter, that He may a - bide.............
poco più animato.
ev - - - er, that He may a - bide with you, with
that He may a - bide with you, with you for - ev - er, with
ev - . - er, that He may a - bide with you for - ev - er, with
.... with you, that He.. may a - bide with you for - ev - .
you for - ev - er, that He may a - bide with
you for - ev - er, that He....... may a - bide with
you for - ev - - er, that He may a - bide with you for-
er, for - ev - er, that He may a - bide with you, may a-

If ye love Me.

you for - ev - - er; e - ven the Spir - it of truth,.. the
you for - ev - er; e - ven the Spir - it of truth,.. the
ev - er, for - ev - - er; e - - ven the Spir - it of truth,.. the
bide for - ev - - er; e - ven the Spir - it of truth,.. the
(Voices alone, ad libitum.)
Spir - it of truth,..... the Spir - it of truth....
Spir - it of truth,..... the Spir - it of... truth.....
Spir - it of truth,..... the Spir - it of truth......
Spir - it of truth,........... the... Spir - it..... of... truth.....
p Organ.
(Voices alone, ad libitum.) cres.
mf tempo 1mo.
If ye love Me,........ keep My com - mand - ments, if ye...
If ye love Me, keep My com - mand - ments, if... ye
If..... ye love Me, keep My... com - mand - ments, if ye
If ye love Me, keep My com - mand - ments, if ye
mf Organ.

love Me,.... keep My command - ments, and I will pray... the Fa - - -
love Me, keep My com-mand-ments, and I will pray the Fa - -
love Me, keep My com-mand-ments, and I will pray the Fa - ther, and
love Me, keep My com-mand - ments, and I............. will pray,..........
ther, and He shall give you an - oth - er... Com - forter, e - ven the
ther, and He shall give you an - oth - er Com - forter, e - ven the
He,....... and He shall give you an - oth - er... Com - forter, e - ven the
...... and He shall give you an - oth - er... Com - forter, e - ven the
Spir - it of truth,..... the Spir - it... of... truth.........
Spir - it of truth,. the Spir - it of truth.........
Spir - it of truth, e - - ven the Spir - it of truth, of... truth.
Spir - it of truth,..... the Spir - it of truth.........

Lord, I call upon Thee.

Psalm cxli. 1, 2.
mæs. ♩ = 84.

The Rev. Sir FREDERICK ARTHUR GORE OUSELEY, Bart., Mus. D. (1825 ——).

sid - - er my voice.... when I... cry..... un - to Thee.
sid - - er my voice when I cry.... un - to Thee. Let my
sid - - er my voice.. when I cry.... un - to Thee.
sid - - er my voice.. when I cry un - to Thee.
pp
Let........ my prayer be.. set.. forth in Thy sight as the in - -
prayer be set forth, be set forth in Thy sight as the in - -
pp
Let my prayer be set forth in Thy sight as the in - -
Let my prayer be set forth in Thy sight as the in - -
cres.
cense, be set forth as the in - cense, and let the lift - ing
cense, be set forth as the in - cense, and let the lift - ing
cres.
cense, be set forth as the in - cense, and let the lift - ing
cense, be set forth as the in - cense, and let the lift - ing
cres.

up of my hands be an eve - ning sac - ri - fice. Lord, I
up of my hands be an eve - ning sac - ri - fice. Lord, I
up of my hands be an eve - ning sac - ri - fice. Lord, I.... call up - on
up of my hands be an eve - ning sac - ri - fice. Lord, I.
call, Lord, I... call, I... call up - on Thee, haste Thee un - to
call, Lord, I... call up - on thee, I call up - on Thee, haste Thee un - to..
Thee, Lord, I call, I... call up - on... Thee, haste Thee un - to
call, Lord, I call, I call up - on Thee, haste Thee un - to
me,......... Lord, I... call up - on...... Thee, haste Thee un - to me,...............
me,......... Lord, I call up - on.... Thee, haste Thee un - to me,... un - to me.
me, Lord, I call up - on..... Thee, haste Thee un - to me, un - to me.
me,......... Lord, I call up - on Thee, haste Thee un - to me, un - to me.

Thine, O Lord, is the Greatness.

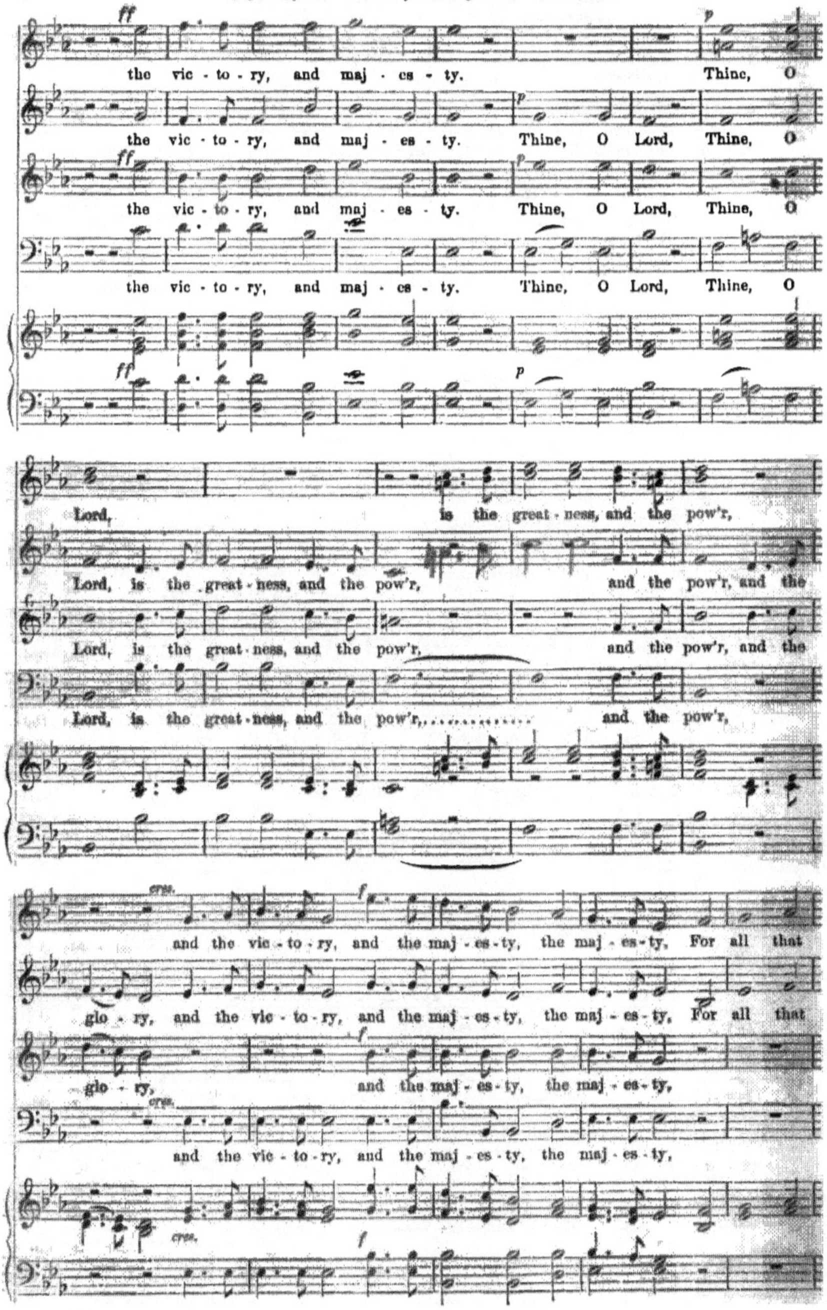
the vic - to - ry, and maj - es - ty. Thine, O
the vic - to - ry, and maj - es - ty. Thine, O Lord, Thine, O
the vic - to - ry, and maj - es - ty. Thine, O Lord, Thine, O
the vic - to - ry, and maj - es - ty. Thine, O Lord, Thine, O
Lord, is the great - ness, and the pow'r,
Lord, is the great - ness, and the pow'r, and the pow'r, and the
Lord, is the great - ness, and the pow'r, and the pow'r, and the
Lord, is the great - ness, and the pow'r, and the pow'r,
and the vic - to - ry, and the maj - es - ty, the maj - es - ty, For all that
glo - ry, and the vic - to - ry, and the maj - es - ty, the maj - es - ty, For all that
glo - ry, and the maj - es - ty, the maj - es - ty,
and the vic - to - ry, and the maj - es - ty, the maj - es - ty,

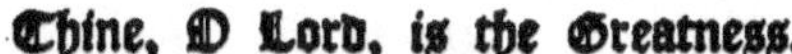

is in the heav'n,........ in the heav'n and the earth are thine.
is in the heav'n,........ in the heav'n and the earth are thine. Thine is the
For all that is in the heav'n and the earth are Thine. Thine is the
For all that is in the heav'n and the earth are Thine. Thine is the
Thine is the king-dom, O.... Lord, and Thou art ex - alt - ed as
king-dom, Thine is the king-dom, O Lord, and Thou art ex - alt - ed as
king-dom, Thine is the king-dom, O...... Lord, and Thou art ex - alt - ed
king-dom, Thine is the king-dom, O Lord, and Thou art ex - alt - ed as
head o - ver all, as head o - ver all, as head, as head o - ver all.
head o - ver all, as head o - ver all, as head, as head o - ver all.
as head o - ver all, as head, as head o - ver all.
head o - ver all, as head o - ver all, as head, as head, o - ver all.

Hear us, O Saviour.

MORITZ HAUPTMANN, Ph. Doc. (1792—1868).

- cor, hear us. To Thee we be - take....... us, to
Suc - cor, hear us. To Thee we....... be - take....... us, to Thee we
Suc - cor, hear us. To Thee we be - take....... us, to Thee we
Suc - cor, hear us. To Thee we
Thee, per - ish - ing chil - dren of A - dam, We turn us, we
turn us, per - ish - ing chil - dren of A - dam, We turn us to Thee, we
turn us, per - ish - ing chil - dren of A - dam, We turn us, we
turn us, per - ish - ing chil - dren of A - dam, We
turn us to Thee, La - ment - - ing and weep - ing, to
turn us to Thee, La - ment - ing and weep - ing,
turn us to Thee, La - ment - ing and weep - - - ing, to
turn us to Thee, La - ment - ing and weep - ing, to

Hear us, O Saviour.

be Thou therefore our De - liv' - rer, be Thou therefore our De - liv' - rer,
be Thou therefore our De - liv' - rer, be Thou therefore our De - liv' - rer, mf
be Thou therefore our De - liv' - rer, be Thou therefore our De - liv' - rer, Look on
be Thou therefore our De - liv' - rer, be Thou therefore our De - liv' - rer,
mf
Look on.. us, in Thy mer-ci-ful kind-ness, Lord, Hear..... our en-
Look.... on us in Thy kind-ness, Lord, O hear our en-
us, on us in.. Thy mer-ci-ful.. kind-ness, Lord, Hear our en-treat....
Look on us, look on us in Thy kind-ness, Lord, O hear our en-
dim. p mf
treat - - ies, And shew us ben-e-dic-tion in this our mis-er-y,
p mf
treat - ies, And shew us ben-e-dic-tion in this our
dim. p mf
- - - ies, And shew us ben-e-dic-tion in this our mis-er-y,
p mf
treat - ies, And shew us ben-e-dic-tion in this our
dim. p mf

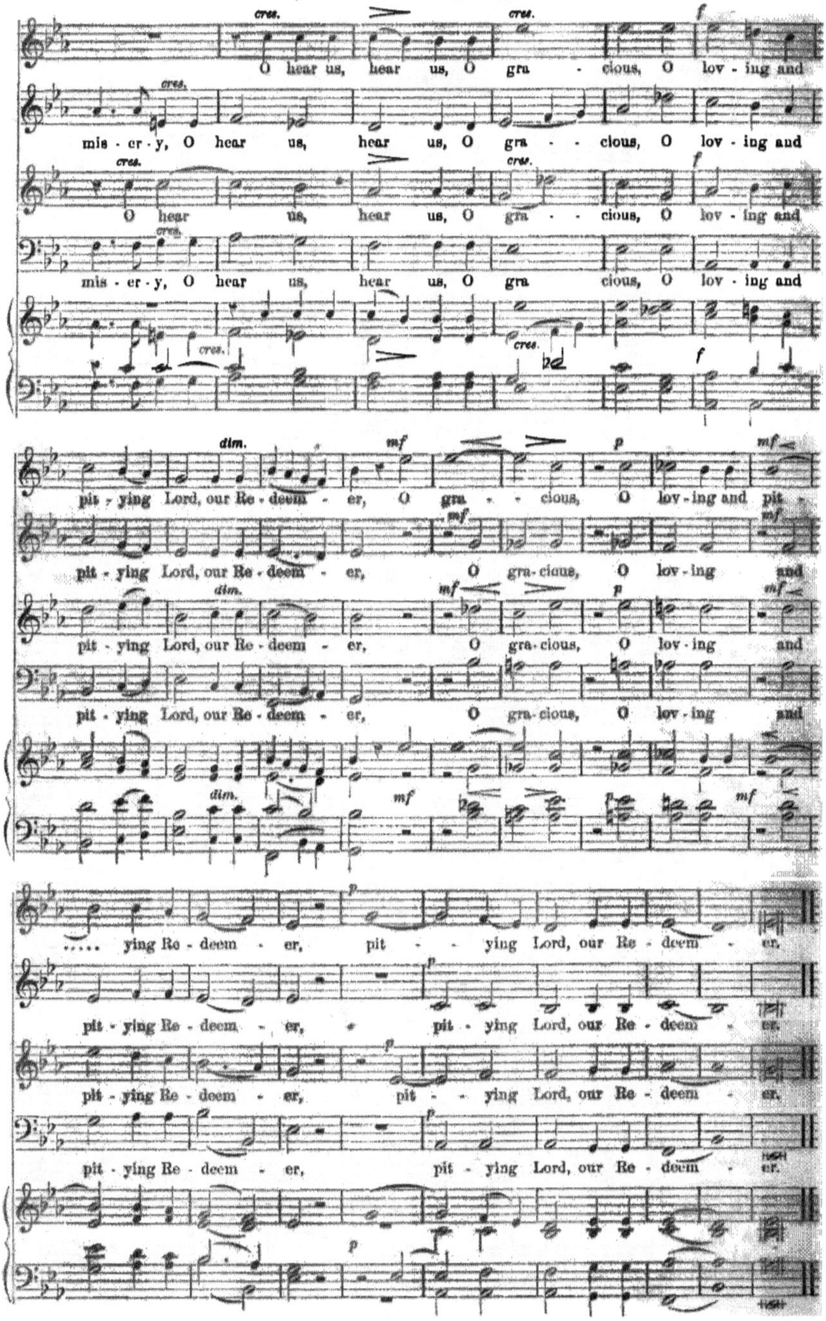
O hear us, hear us, O gra - cious, O lov - ing and
mis - er - y, O hear us, hear us, O gra - - cious, O lov - ing and
O hear us, hear us, O gra - - cious, O lov - ing and
mis - er - y, O hear us, hear us, O gra cious, O lov - ing and
pit - ying Lord, our Re - deem - er, O gra - - cious, O lov - ing and pit -
pit - ying Lord, our Re - deem - er, O gra - cious, O lov - ing and
pit - ying Lord, our Re - deem - er, O gra - cious, O lov - ing and
pit - ying Lord, our Re - deem - er, O gra - cious, O lov - ing and
..... ying Re - deem - er, pit - - ying Lord, our Re - deem - er,
pit - ying Re - deem - er, pit - ying Lord, our Re - deem - er.
pit - ying Re - deem - er, pit - - ying Lord, our Re - deem - er.
pit - ying Re - deem - er, pit - ying Lord, our Re - deem - er.

PSALM lxxxvii.
Andante.
FRIEDRICH HEINRICH HIMMEL (1765—1814).
p
mf
8va
SOLO.
In - cline Thine Ear, in - cline Thine Ear to me,.. in - cline..... Thine Ear,..... in-
cline Thine Ear to.. me,.. O Lord, make haste to de - liv - er me. In-
dim.
cres.
dim.
cline Thine Ear,.... in-cline Thine Ear to me,.. O Lord, make haste, make haste to de-
p
liv - er... me. O save me for Thy mer - cies' sake, O save....... me
cres.
p

Incline Thine Ear to me.

cline Thine Ear,..... in-cline Thine Ear to me,.. O Lord, make haste, make
cline Thine Ear, in-cline Thine Ear to... me, O Lord, make haste, make
In-cline Thine Ear, in-cline Thine Ear to... me, O Lord, make haste, make haste to de-
cline Thine Ear............ to me,
haste to de-liv-er me, O save me for Thy mer-cies' sake, O save...... me,
haste to de-liv er me, O save me for Thy mer-cies' sake, O save....... me,
liv-er me, O save me for Thy mer-cies' sake, save, O
O............ Lord,........................... for Thy mer-cies' sake, O
save me for Thy mer-cies' sake.
save me for Thy mer-cies' sake.
save me for Thy mer-cies' sake.
save me for Thy mer-cies' sake.
mf

Sweet is Thy Mercy.

THE REV. JOHN SAMUEL BEWLEY MONSELL, L.L.D. (1811—1875), 1863.

JOSEPH BARNBY (1838 ——).

sweet, and find Thy mer - cy sweet, Thy mer - cy sweet.
VERSE—Soprano. p a tempo.
Light Thou our wea - ry
VERSE—Alto. p
Light Thou our wea - ry
VERSE—Tenor. p
Light Thou our wea - ry
VERSE—Bass. p
Light Thou our wea - ry
Lead Thou my wand'ring feet; Sweet, sweet is Thy
way, our wand - 'ring feet; That while we stay on earth we may Still
way, Lead Thou our wand - 'ring feet; That while we stay on earth we may Still
way; Lead Thou our wand'ring feet; That while we stay on earth we may Still
way, our wand - 'ring feet; That while on earth we may

19

Sweet is Thy Mercy.

Thy mer-cy sweet, my joy,....... Thy mer-cy sweet, my joy, Thy mer-cy
mer-cy sweet, our joy,....... our joy,... Thy mer-cy
mer-cy sweet, our joy, our joy, Thy mer-cy, mer-cy
mer-cy sweet, our joy, our joy, Thy....... mer-cy
mer-cy sweet, our joy, our joy, Thy mer-cy
mf f ff
sweet. A - men,............... A - men, A - men.
mf ff
sweet. A - men, A - men.
mf ff
sweet. A - men, A - men.
mf ff
sweet. A - men, A - men.
mf ff
sweet A - men, A - men.
mf cres. ff

The Lord is my Shepherd.

Psalm XXIII. 1—4, 6.

GEORGE ALEXANDER MACFARREN, Mus. D. (1813 —).

stor - eth, re - stor - eth my soul, He leadeth me in the paths,... the paths,..... of
stor - eth, re - stor - eth my soul, He leadeth me in the paths, the paths of
stor - eth, re - stor - eth my soul, He leadeth me in the paths, the paths of
re - stor - eth my soul, the paths of
right - eous - ness, for His Name's........ sake,...... His Name's.. sake. Yea, though I
right - eous - ness, His Name's sake. Yea, though I
right - eous - ness, for His Name's........ sake,........ Name's sake. Yea, though I
right - eous - ness, for His Name's sake,...... His Name's sake. Yea, though I
walk thro' the val - ley of the shad - ow of death, Yea, though I
walk thro' the val - ley of the shad - ow of death, Yea, though I
walk thro' the val - ley, Yea, though I
walk thro' the val - ley of the shad - - - ow of death, Yea, though I

The Lord is my Shepherd.

sure - ly good - ness and mer - cy shall fol - low me all the days of my
sure - ly good - ness and mer - cy shall fol - low me.. all the days of my
sure - ly good - ness and mer - cy shall fol - low me all the days of my
sure - ly good - ness and mer - cy shall fol - low me all the days of my
life, and I will dwell in the house of the Lord.... for ev - er, I will dwell in the
life, and I will dwell in the house of the Lord for ev - er, I will dwell in the
life, and I will dwell in the house of the Lord for ev - er, I will dwell in the
life, and I will dwell in the house of the Lord.... for ev - er, I will dwell in the
house of the Lord for ev - er, for ev - er, for ev - - - - er.
house of the Lord for ev - er, for ev - er, for ev - - - - er.
house of the Lord for ev - er, for ev - er, for ev - - - - er.
house of the Lord for ev - er, for ev - - - - er.

In Thee, O Lord, have I put my Trust.

me, bow down Thine Ear to me, bow down Thine Ear, Thine
Ear to me,.... to me, bow down Thine
Ear to me,.............. Thine Ear.......... ..
Ear to me, bow down Thine Ear to me, bow down Thine
Ear to me, bow down Thine Ear to me, bow down Thine Ear to
Ear to me, bow down Thine Ear to me, bow down Thine Ear to
.... to me, bow down Thine Ear to me, bow down Thine
Ear to me, bow down Thine
me, to.... me, make haste, make haste to de - liv - er
me,.... to.... me, make haste, make haste to de - liv - er
Ear to..... me, make haste, make haste to de - liv - er
Ear......... to me, make haste, make haste to de - liv - er
p
pp
dim
Ped.
cres.

In Thee, O Lord, have I put my Trust.

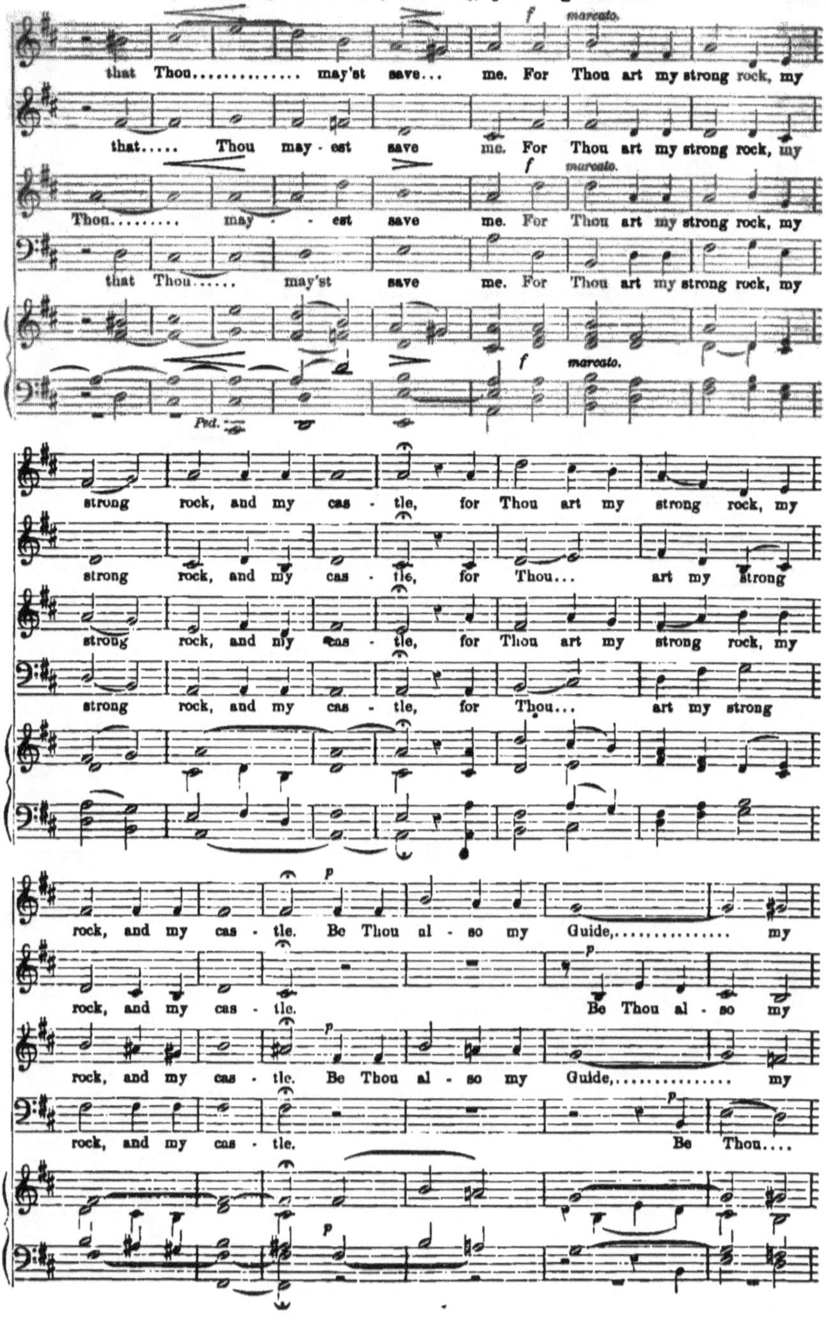
f marcato.
that Thou.............. may'st save... me. For Thou art my strong rock, my
that..... Thou may - est save me. For Thou art my strong rock, my
f marcato.
Thou......... may - - est save me. For Thou art my strong rock, my
that Thou...... may'st save me. For Thou art my strong rock, my
f marcato.
Ped.
strong rock, and my cas - tle, for Thou art my strong rock, my
strong rock, and my cas - tle, for Thou... art my strong
strong rock, and my cas - tle, for Thou art my strong rock, my
strong rock, and my cas - tle, for Thou... art my strong
p
rock, and my cas - tle. Be Thou al - so my Guide,............... my
p
rock, and my cas - tle. Be Thou al - so my
p
rock, and my cas - tle. Be Thou al - so my Guide,............... my
p
rock, and my cas - tle. Be Thou....
p

In Thee, O Lord, have I put my Trust.

Not unto us, O Lord.

THOMAS ATTWOOD WALMISLEY, Mus. D. (1814—1856).

Not unto us, O Lord.

Al - le - lu - ia! Al - le - lu - ia! Al - le - lu - ia!
Al - le - lu - ia! Al - le - lu - ia! Al -
Al - le - lu - ia! Al - le - lu - ia! Al - le - lu - ia!
Al - le - lu - ia! Al - le - lu - ia! Al - le - lu - ia!
Al - le - lu - ia! Al - le - lu - ia! Al - le - lu - ia! Al - le - lu - ia! Al -
le - lu - ia! Al - le - lu - ia! Al - le - lu - ia! Al - le - lu - ia! Al
Al - le - lu - ia! Al - le - lu - ia! Al - le - lu - ia! Al - le - lu - ia! Al -
Al - le - lu - ia! Al - le - lu - ia! Al - le - lu - ia! Al - le -
le - lu - ia! Al - le - lu - ia! Al - le - lu - ia! A - men.
le - lu - ia! Al - le - lu - ia! Al - le - lu - ia! Al - le - lu - ia! A - men.
le - lu - ia! Al - le - lu - ia! Al - le - lu - ia! Al - le - lu - ia! A - men.
lu - ia! Al - le - lu - ia! Al - le - lu - ia! A - men.

O love the Lord.

PSALM XXXI. 26, 27.

SIR ARTHUR SEYMOUR SULLIVAN, Mus. D. (1842——).

p Smoothly, and not too slow. ♩ = 80.*

* Original key, E.

do - er, re - ward - eth the proud do - er.
proud do - er, re - ward - eth the proud do - er.
plen - teous - ly re - ward - eth the proud do - er.
plen - teous - ly re - ward - eth the proud do - er. Be strong, and
Be strong, and He shall es - tab - lish your heart, all ye that
Be strong, and He shall es - tab - lish your heart, all ye that
Be strong, and He shall es - tab - lish your heart, all ye that
He shall es - tab - lish, es - tab - lish your heart, all ye that
put your trust in the Lord, And He shall es - tab - lish your
put your trust in the Lord, And He shall es - tab - lish, es - tab - lish your
put your trust in the Lord, And He shall es -
put your trust in the Lord, And
f
dim
f
f
sempre f
sempre f
sempre f
sempre f

O love the Lord.

plen - teous-ly,..... and plen - teous-ly... re - ward - - eth the
faith-ful, and plen - teous-ly re - ward - - - - eth the
them that are faith-ful, and plen-teous-ly re - ward - - eth the
them that are faith-ful, and plen - teous - ly re - ward-eth the
proud...... do - er. O...... love.. the Lord,.. all
proud...... do - er. O..... love,.. O love... the Lord,.. all
proud do - er. O..... love,.. O love... the Lord, all
proud........... do - er........... all
ye His saints,.......... O.... love the Lord. A - - - - men.
ye His saints, O love the Lord. A - - - - men.
ye... His saints, O love the Lord. A - - - men.
ye... His saints, O love the Lord. A - - - men.

Out of the Deep have I called unto Thee.

Psalm cxxx.
Larghetto.

Johannes Chrysostomus Wolfgang Theophilus (Gottlieb or Amadeus) Mozart (1756—1791).

DUET.
well the voice, the voice.... of my.... com - plaint. O let Thine
O let Thine
Ears con - - sid - - er.... well the voice, the voice of my.... com-
Ears con - - sid - er well the voice of my..... com-
CHORUS.
plaint ; O let Thine Ears con - - sid - - er.... well the voice, the
plaint ; O let Thine Ears con - - sid - er well the voice, the
let Thine Ears con - - sid - - er well the voice, the
con - sid - er well the voice, the

Out of the Deep have I called unto Thee.

DUET.
may, who may.. a-bide it? For there is mer-cy, is mer-cy with Thee, there-
For there is mer-cy, mer-cy with Thee,
CHORUS.
fore.. shalt Thou, shalt Thou... be fear-ed, For there is mer-cy, is
there-fore shalt Thou.... be fear-ed, For there is mer-cy, is
there is mer-cy, is
mer - cy with Thee, there-fore shalt Thou, shalt Thou, be fear-ed.
mer - cy with Thee, there-fore shalt Thou, shalt Thou.... be fear-ed.
mer - cy with Thee, there-fore shalt Thou, shalt Thou.... be fear-ed.
there is mer-cy with Thee, there-fore shalt Thou, shalt Thou.... be fear-ed.

Lord, how long wilt Thou forget me?

PARAPHRASE FROM PSALM XIII.   JAKOB LUDWIG FELIX MENDELSSOHN-BARTHOLDY, Ph. D. (1809—1847).

Andante. ♩ = 76.

cres.
While in lone-ly grief I mourn? And how long Thy Face be hid-ing?
While in lone-ly grief I mourn? And how long Thy Face be hid-ing?
While in lone-ly... grief I mourn? And how long............ Thy Face be hid-ing?
While in lone-ly grief I mourn? And how long Thy Face be hid-ing?
f dim. p
Nev-er-more, nev-er-more, Wilt Thou nev-er-more re-turn?
Nev-er-more, nev-er-more, Wilt Thou nev-er-more re-turn?
f dim. p
Nev-er-more, nev-er-more, Wilt Thou nev-er-more re-turn?
Nev-er-more, nev-er-more, Wilt Thou nev-er-more re-turn?
SOLO.
Lord, how long must I.... take coun-sel, Hav-ing sor-row in my heart?.....

 Lord, how long wilt Thou forget me?

sor - row in my heart? Foes re - lent - less rise a - gainst me, And no
sor - row in my heart? Foes re - lent - less rise a - gainst me, And no
sor - row in my heart? Foes re - lent - less rise a - gainst me,
sor - row in my heart? Foes re - lent - less rise a - gainst me, And no
help - er take my part? O Lord, O Lord,
SOLO.
help - er take my part? O Lord, O Lord, Lord............
And none take my part? O Lord, O Lord,
help - er take my part? O Lord, O Lord,
pp
p
.... how long wilt Thou for - get me While in lone - ly grief I mourn?

TUTTI. cres.
And how long Thy Face be hid-ing? Wilt Thou nev-er-more re-turn?
And how long Thy Face be hid-ing? Wilt Thou nev-er-more re-turn?
And how long Thy Face be hid-ing? Wilt Thou nev-er-more re-turn?
And how long Thy Face be hid-ing? Wilt Thou nev-er-more re-turn?
SOLO.
Wilt Thou nev-er-more re-turn? nev-er-more, nev-er-more,
pp
pp
SOLO.
nev-er-more?
pp
Nev-er-more?
pp
Nev-er-more?
Nev-er-more?
pp

Psalm v. 1, 2.

LANGDON COLBORNE, Mus. B., Cantab. (1837 ——).

Ponder my Words, O Lord.

call - ing, for to Thee will I make my.. pray'r...... Pon - der my words, O
call - ing, for to Thee will I make my pray'r, Pon - der my words, O
call - ing, for to Thee will I make my pray'r...... Pon - - - der my
voice of my call - ing, to Thee will I make my pray'r...... Pon - - - der my
Lord, con - sid - er my med - i - ta - tion. O
Lord,............ con - sid - er my med - i - ta - tion, O
words, O Lord, con - sid - er my med - i - ta - tion, O
words, O...... Lord, con - sid - er my med - i - ta - tion, O
heark - en Thou to the voice of my call - ing, my King and my God.
heark - en Thou to the voice of my call - ing, my King and my God.
heark - en Thou to the voice of my call - ing, my King.. and my God.
heark - en Thou to the voice of my call - ing, my King and my God.

I will lay me down in Peace.

Ps. iv. 9.

HENRY GADSBY (1842 ——)

Andante con moto. ♩ = 72.

on - ly Thou That mak - est me dwell in safe - - ty, That
on - ly Thou. That mak - est me dwell in safe - - ty, That
on - ly Thou That mak - est me dwell in safe - - ty, That
on - ly Thou, 'tis on - - - - - ly Thou That
mak - est me dwell in safe - ty. I will lay me down in peace, I will
mak - est me dwell in safe - ty. I will lay me down in peace, I will
mak - est me dwell in safe - ty. I will lay me down in peace, I will
mak - est me dwell in safe - ty. I will lay me down in
lay me down in peace, I will lay me down in peace, in peace.
lay me down in peace,.... I will lay me down in peace,
lay me down in peace, I will lay me down.... in
peace, and take my rest,.... will lay me down in

I will lay me down in Peace.

cres - cen - do. f dim.
on - ly, for it is Thou, Lord, on - ly, That mak - est me dwell in safe - ty,
on - ly, for it is Thou, Lord, on - ly, That mak - est me dwell,......
cres - cen - do. f dim.
on - ly, for it is Thou, Lord, on - ly, That mak - est me dwell,............
on - ly, for it is Thou, Lord, on - - ly, That
cres - cen - do. f dim.
p pp
mak - est me dwell in safe - - ty. I will
mak - est me dwell in safe - - ty. I will
p pp
mak - est me dwell in safe - ty. I will
mak - est me dwell in safe - - ty. I will
p
dim. rall.
lay............... me down............ in peace.
lay............... me down............ in peace.
dim. rall.
lay............... me down............ in peace.
lay............... me down............ in peace.
dim. rall.

O how amiable are Thy Dwellings.

JOSEPH BARNBY (1838 ——).

courts of the house of the Lord: my heart and my flesh re - joice in the
courts of the house of the Lord: my heart and my flesh re - joice in the
courts of the house of the Lord: the liv - ing
house of the Lord, the
Ped.
dim. cres. e rall.
Lord, re - joice in the liv - ing God
Lord, re - joice in the liv - ing God
dim. f cres e rall.
God, my heart and my flesh re - joice in the Lord.
Lord, the liv - ing God
dim. cres e rall.
ff tempo 1mo.
O how a - mia - ble are Thy dwell - ings: Thou Lord, Thou Lord of hosts!
O how a - mia - ble are Thy dwell - ings: Thou Lord, Thou Lord of hosts!
ff
O how a - mia - ble are Thy dwell - ings: Thou Lord, Thou Lord of hosts!
O how a - mia - ble are Thy dwell - ings: Thou Lord, Thou Lord of hosts!
tempo 1mo.

O how amiable are Thy Dwellings.

al - - way, al - way prais - ing Thee......
al - way, al - way prais - ing Thee......
O how a - mia - ble are Thy dwell - ings: Thou Lord, Thou Lord of hosts! O...
O how a - mia - ble are Thy dwell - ings: Thou Lord, Thou Lord of hosts!
O how a - mia - ble are Thy dwell - ings: Thou Lord, Thou Lord of hosts!
O how a - mia - ble are Thy dwell - ings: Thou Lord, Thou Lord of hosts!
...... how a - mia - ble are Thy dwell - ings: Thou Lord, Thou Lord of hosts! My
O how a - mia - ble are Thy dwell - ings: Thou Lord, Thou Lord of hosts!
O how a - mia - ble are Thy dwell - ings: Thou Lord, Thou Lord of hosts!
O how a - mia - ble are Thy dwell - ings: Thou Lord, Thou Lord of hosts!

O how amiable are Thy Dwellings.

ff Maestoso. ♩ = 72.
Glo - ry be to the Fa - ther, and to the Son, and to the Ho - ly
Glo - ry be to the Fa - ther, and to the Son, and to the Ho - ly
ff
Glo - ry be to the Fa - ther, and to the Son, and to the Ho - ly
Glo - ry be to the Fa - ther, and to the Son, and to the Ho - ly
ff
Ghost; As it was in the be - gin - ning, is now, and ev - er
Ghost; ... As it was in the be - gin - ning, is now, and ev - er
Ghost; As it was in the be - gin - ning, is now, and ev - er
Ghost; As it was in the be - gin - ning, is now, and ev - er
rit.
shall be, world with - out end. A - men, A - men.
shall be, world with - out end. A - men, A - men.
rit.
shall be, world with - out end. A - men, A - men.
shall be, world with - out end. A - men, A - men.
rit.

The Lord is my Shepherd.

PSALM XXIII.

CARYL FLORIO (1843 ——), 1881.

Moderato, ma con moto.

Lord is my Shep - herd, therefore can I lack noth - ing. He..... shall...
Shep - herd, there - - fore can I lack noth - ing. He shall...
Lord is my Shep - herd, therefore can I lack noth - ing.
mp sempre tranquillamente.
The Lord is my Shep - herd, my Shep - herd. He shall
mp
feed me in a green.. pas - ture, and lead...... me forth...... be -
feed me in a green pas - ture, and lead...... me forth...... be -
He shall feed me in a green.. pas - ture, and lead...... me forth...... be -
feed me in a green.. pas - ture, and lead...... me forth...... be -
side the waters of com - fort, the waters of com - fort......
side the waters of com - fort, the waters of com - fort......
side the waters of com - fort, the waters of com - fort......
side the waters of com - fort, the waters of com - fort......

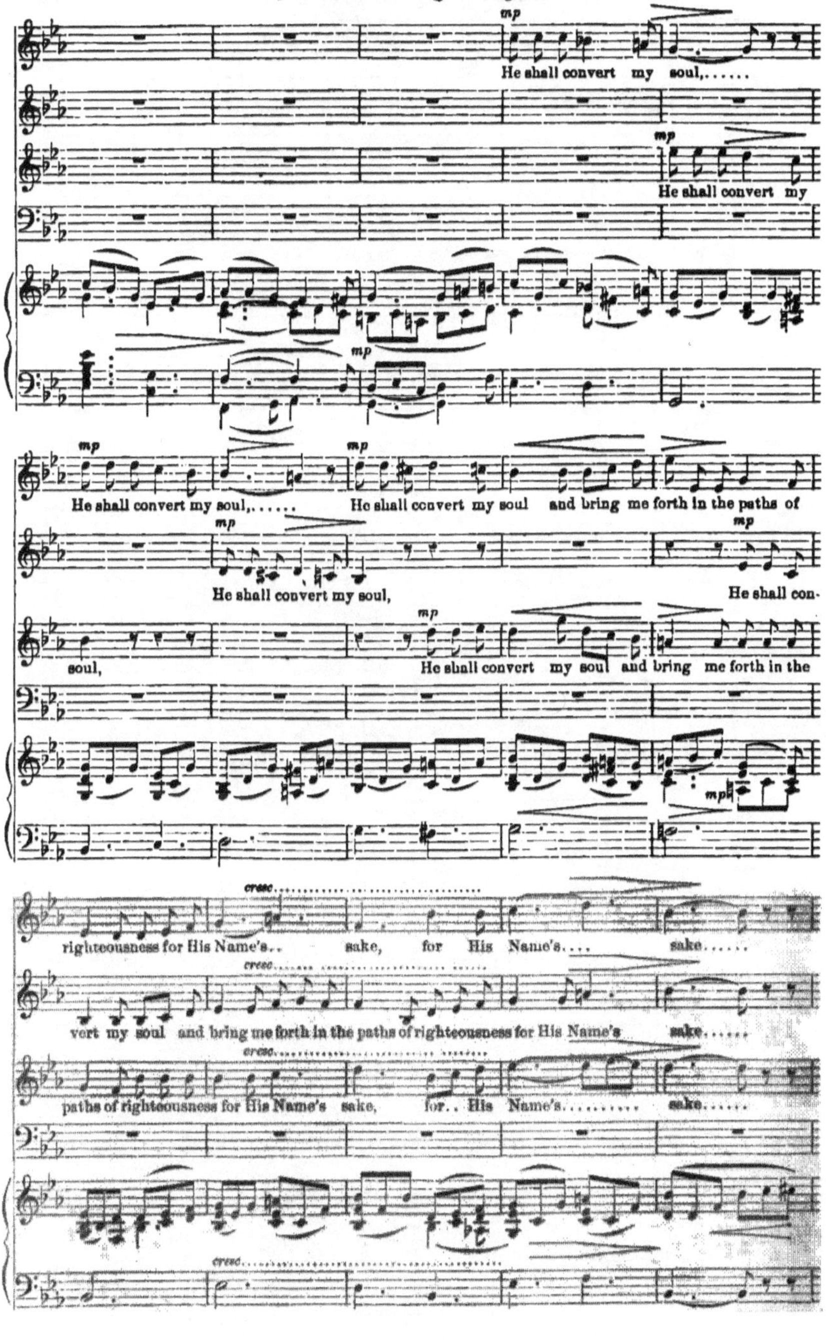
He shall convert my soul,......
He shall convert my
He shall convert my soul,...... He shall convert my soul and bring me forth in the paths of
He shall convert my soul, He shall con-
soul, He shall convert my soul and bring me forth in the
righteousness for His Name's.. sake, for His Name's.... sake......
vert my soul and bring me forth in the paths of righteousness for His Name's sake......
paths of righteousness for His Name's sake, for.. His Name's.......... sake......
mp
cresc.

Yea, though I walk through the val - ley of the shad - ow of death,....
I will fear no..... e - vil; for
I will fear no...... e - vil; for
I will fear no e - vil; for
I will fear no e - vil; for
Thou art with me;...
Thou art with me;.. Thy rod and Thy staff. they com - - - fort
Thou art with me;.. Thy rod and Thy staff. they com - - - fort
Thou art with me;.... Thy rod and Thy staff. they com - fort

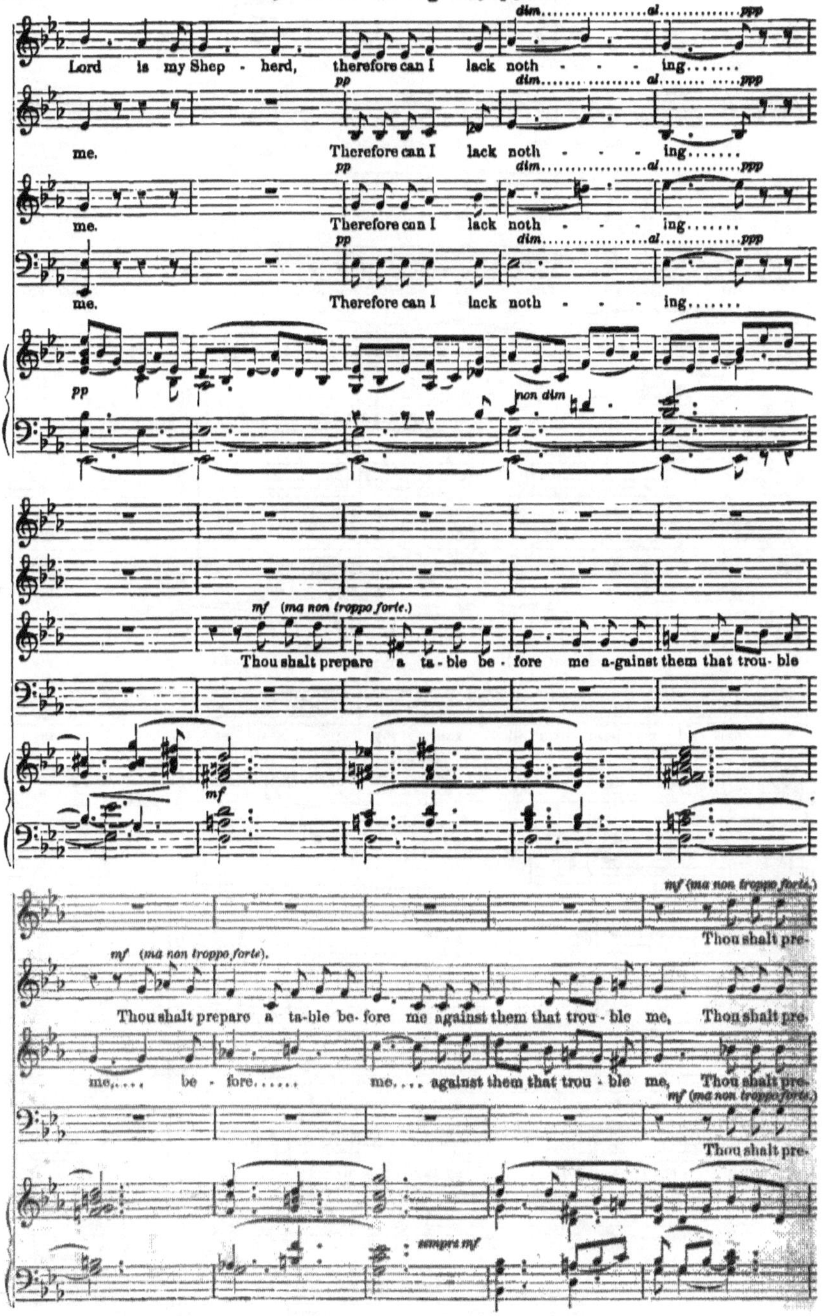
dim. al ppp
Lord is my Shep - herd, therefore can I lack noth - - - - ing.......
pp dim. al ppp
me. Therefore can I lack noth - - - - ing.......
pp dim. al ppp
me. Therefore can I lack noth - - - - ing.......
pp dim. al ppp
me. Therefore can I lack noth - - - - ing.......
pp
non dim
mf (ma non troppo forte.)
Thou shalt prepare a ta - ble be - fore me a-gainst them that trou - ble
mf
mf (ma non troppo forte.)
Thou shalt pre-
mf (ma non troppo forte).
Thou shalt prepare a ta-ble be-fore me against them that trou - ble me, Thou shalt pre-
me,..... be - fore...... me..... against them that trou - ble me, Thou shalt pre-
mf (ma non troppo forte.)
Thou shalt pre-
sempre mf

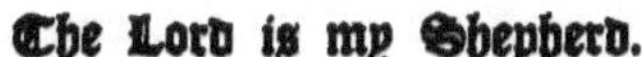

pare a ta-ble be-fore me a-gainst them that trou-ble me. Thou hast an-
pare a ta-ble be-fore me a-gainst them that trou-ble me. Thou hast an-
pare a ta-ble be-fore me a-gainst them that trou-ble me. Thou hast an-
pare a ta-ble be-fore me a-gainst them that trou-ble me. Thou hast an-
oint-ed my head with oil, and my cup shall be full, my
oint-ed my head with oil, and my cup shall be full, my
oint-ed my head with oil, and my cup shall be full, my
oint-ed my head with oil, and my cup shall be full, my
cup shall be full,...... my cup shall be full. But Thy
cup shall be full,...... my cup shall be full. But Thy
cup shall be full,...... my cup shall be full. But Thy
cup shall be full,...... my cup shall be full. But Thy
mp
cresc
al
f
mp
dim.

The Lord is my Shepherd.

life,..... and I...... will dwell in the house of the Lord for ev - er, for
life,..... and I...... will dwell in the house of the Lord for ev - er, for
life,..... and I...... will dwell in the house of the Lord for ev - er, for
life,..... and I...... will dwell in the house of the Lord for ev - er, for
poco dim............. p dim - - - in - - - u - en - do.
ev - er and ev - er, for ev - - - er, for ev - - -
poco dim.......... p dim - - - in - - - u - en - do.
ev - er and ev - - - er, for ev - - - er, for ev - - -
poco dim............ p dim - - - in - - - u - en - do.
ev - er and ev - er, for ev - - - er, for ev - - -
poco dim............ p dim - - - in - - - u - en - do.
ev - er and ev - er, for ev - - - er, for ev - - -
poco dim.............. p dim - - - in - - - u - en -
pp Ped.
er.........pp
er.........
Tenor.   pp
er.........
Bass. er.........pp
pp
do...... al..... fine.
pp

I waited patiently for the Lord.

f marcato.
heard my call - - ing..... He brought me al - so out of the hor - ri - ble
heard my call - - ing..... He brought me al - so out of the hor - ri - ble
heard my call - - ing. He brought me al - so out of the hor - ri - ble
heard my call - - ing..... He brought me al - so out of the hor - ri - ble
f marcato.
pit,... out of the mire and clay, out of the mire and clay, and set my
pit,... out of the mire, out of the mire and clay, and set my
pit,... out of the mire and clay, out of the mire and clay, and set my
pit,.. out of the mire, out of the mire and clay, and set my
ff
foot up - on the rock, and or - der - ed.. my go - - ings, and set my foot up-
foot up - on the rock, and or - der - ed my go - - ings, and set my foot up-
foot up - on the rock, and or - der - ed.. my go - - ings, and set my foot up-
foot up - on the rock, and or - der - ed.. my go - - ings, and set my foot up-

I waited patiently for the Lord.

dolce. pp
And He hath put.......... a new
And He hath put.......... a new
dolce. pp
un - to our God, our God;..... And He hath put.......... a new
And He hath put.......... a new
song in my mouth,... in my mouth, e - ven a thanks - giv - ing
song in my mouth,... in my mouth, e - ven a thanks - giv - ing
song in my mouth, in my mouth,... e - ven a thanks - giv - ing
song in my mouth, in my mouth, e - ven a thanks - giv - ing
crescendo.
p
un - to our God,......... un - to our God:.........
p
un - to our God,......... un - to
p
un - to.... our God,......... un - to our God:.........
p
un - to our God,......... un - to

I waited patiently for the Lord.

trust,...... their trust.. in.. the Lord,...... and shall put their trust,.... their trust
and shall put their trust,.... their trust
and shall put their trust,...... and shall put their trust,... their trust
and shall put their trust,.... their trust
cres-cen-do.
in the Lord, and shall put their trust, their trust in the Lord, their trust in the
in the Lord, and shall put their trust, their trust in the Lord, their trust in the
in the Lord, and shall put their trust, their trust in the Lord, their trust in the
in the Lord, and shall put their trust, their trust in the Lord, their trust in the
ri - tard - an - do.
Lord, their trust,... their trust in the Lord... A - - - men.....
Lord, their trust.... in the Lord... A - - - men.....
Lord, their trust. in the Lord... A - - - men...
Lord, their trust.... in the Lord A - - men.....
mf ri - tard - an - do.

Call to Remembrance, O Lord.

PSALM xxv. 5, 6.

RICHARD FARRANT (1530?—1580).
The Organ Part by VINCENT NOVELLO (1781—1861).

which hath been ev - er of.... old. O.... re - mem - ber not the sins and of -
old, which hath been ev - er of old. O.... re - mem - ber not the sins and of -
which hath been ev - er of...... old. O.... re - mem - ber not the sins and of -
old, which hath been ev - er of old. O.... re - mem - ber not the sins and of -
fen - ces of my youth, but ac - cord - ing to Thy mer - cy think Thou on me, O Lord;
fen - ces of my youth, but ac - cord ing to Thy...... mer - cy think Thou on me, O Lord; but ac -
fen - ces of my youth, but ac - cord - ing to Thy mer - - cy.... think Thou on me, O Lord; but ac -
fen - ces of my youth, but ac cord - ing to Thy mer - cy.... think Thou on me, O Lord; but ac -
but ac - cord - ing to Thy mer - cy think Thou on me, O Lord, for.. Thy good - ness.....
cord - ing to Thy...... mer - cy think Thou on me, O Lord, for.. Thy good - ness.....
cord - ing to Thy mer - - cy.... think Thou on me, O Lord, for... Thy good - ness.....
cord - ing to Thy mer - cy... think Thou on me, O Lord, for.. Thy good - ness.....

Comfort, O Lord, the Soul of Thy Servant.

Lord, the soul of Thy serv-ant, for un-to Thee do I lift up my soul, do I
Lord, the soul of Thy serv-ant, for un-to Thee do I.... lift up my soul, do I
Lord, the soul of Thy serv-ant, for un-to Thee do I.... lift up my soul, do I
Lord, the soul of Thy serv-ant, for un-to Thee do I lift up my soul, do I
lift up my soul. Com-fort, O Lord, the soul of Thy serv-ant, for un-to
lift up my soul. Com-fort, O Lord, the soul of Thy serv-ant, for un-to
lift up my soul. Com-fort, O Lord, the soul of Thy serv-ant, for un-to
lift up my soul. Com-fort, O Lord, the soul of Thy serv-ant, for un-to
Thee do I lift up my soul, do I lift up my soul.
Thee do I..... lift up my soul, do I lift up my.... soul.
Thee do I.... lift up my soul, do I lift up my....... soul.
Thee do I lift up my soul, do I lift up my soul.
Repeat as CHORUS. p VERSE. f CHORUS.
cres. dim.
8ves. ad lib.

Alphabetical Index.

Index according to the Christian Year.

Biographical Index.

ALLEN, GEORGE BENJAMIN, Mus. B., Oxon., 1852. Son of Mr. Benjamin Allen. Born in London, 1822.

Chorister in Westminster Abbey; a Member of the Choir of Armagh Cathedral, 1848—1862; Organist and Choirmaster of All Saints' Church, Kensington Park, London; of Toorak Church, Melbourne, 1870—1871.

68.*

ATTWOOD, THOMAS. Born in London, 1767. Died at Chelsea, 1838.

Chorister in the Chapel Royal; Organist of St. George the Martyr, Queen Square, London; Organist of St. Paul's Cathedral, London, 1796; Composer to the Chapel Royal, 1796; Organist of King George IV.'s private Chapel at Brighton, 1821; Organist of the Chapel Royal, 1836.

96, 98, 154, 267.

BARNBY, JOSEPH. Son of Mr. Thomas Barnby. Born at York, 1838.

Chorister in York Minster; Organist of St. Andrew's, Wells Street, London, 1863—1872; Precentor and Organist of Eton College, 1875.

3, 14, 38, 55, 150, 163, 262, 288, 324.

BENNETT, SIR WILLIAM STERNDALE, Mus. D., Cantab., 1856; D.C.L., Oxon., 1870. Son of Robert Bennett, an organist at Sheffield. Born at Sheffield, 1816. Died at London, 1875.

Chorister in King's College Chapel, Cambridge, 1824—1826; Professor of Music in the University of Cambridge, 1856; Principal of the Royal Academy of Music, 1866; received knighthood, 1871.

85.

CALKIN, JOHN BAPTISTE. Son of James Calkin, a musician and composer. Born in London, 1827.

Organist of the College of St. Columba, near Dublin, 1846—1853; of St. Thomas' Church, Camden New Town, London.

190, 216.

COLBORNE, LANGDON, Mus. B., Cantab., 1864. Son of Mr. Thomas Colborne. Born at Hackney, Middlesex, 1837.

Organist of St. Michael's College, Tenbury, 1860; of Beverly Minster, 1874; of Wigan Parish Church, 1875; of Dorking Parish Church, 1877; and of Hereford Cathedral, 1877.

317.

---

* The numbers refer to the page on which the anthem may be found.

CORNELL, JOHN HENRY. Born May 8, 1828, in New York City.

Was for many years Organist at St. Paul's Chapel (Trinity Parish) in that city, in which he still resides, devoting himself chiefly to the preparation of works of a theoretical and educational nature. His "Primer of Modern Musical Tonality" (1876), has attained considerable popularity.

173.

CROTCH, WILLIAM, Mus. D., Oxon,, 1799. Born at Norwich, 1775. Died at Taunton, 1847.

Organist of Christ Church, Oxford, 1790; of St. John's College, and Professor of Music in the University of Oxford, 1797; Principal of the Royal Academy of Music, 1822.

346.

ELVEY, Sir GEORGE JOB, Mus. D., Oxon., 1840. Born at Canterbury, 1816.

Chorister in Canterbury Cathedral; Organist of St. George's Chapel, Windsor, 1835; received knighthood, 1871.

10, 129, 147, 170, 204.

FARRANT, RICHARD, born cir. 1530. Died, 1580.

Gentleman of the Chapel Royal, 15··—1564, and 1569—1580; Master of the Choristers of St. George's Chapel, Windsor, 1564—1569.

The Anthem, "Lord, for Thy tender Mercies' Sake," is commonly ascribed to him, but without sufficient grounds. It is attributed by several authorities to JOHN HILTON, Organist of St. Margaret's, Westminster, who died about the middle of the 17th century.

94, 344.

FLORIO, CARYL. Born in Tavistock, Devonshire, England, November 3d, 1843.

Came to the United States in September, 1858. During 1856—1860 was widely celebrated (under the family name of ROBJOHN) as one of the finest boy-soloists ever heard in Trinity Church, New York. He is now well known as a composer, a conductor, a pianist, and an organist.

330.

GADSBY, HENRY. Born at Hackney, London, 1842.

Chorister in St. Paul's Cathedral, London, 1849—1858; Organist of St. Peter's, Brockley, Surrey.

62, 236, 243, 320.

GARRETT, GEORGE MURSELL, Mus. D., Cantab., 1867; M. A. *honoris causa*, 1878. Son of William Garrett, Master of the Choristers of Winchester Cathedral. Born at Winchester, 1834.

Chorister at New College, Oxford; Assistant Organist of Winchester Cathedral, 1851; Organist of Madras Cathedral, 1854; Organist of St. John's College, Cambridge, 1857, and to the University, 1872.

157.

GOSS, Sir JOHN, Mus. D., Cantab., 1876. Son of Joseph Goss, Organist of Fareham, Hampshire. Born at Fareham, 1800. Died at Brixton, London, 1880.

Chorister in the Chapel Royal, 1811; Organist of St. Luke's, Chelsea, circa 1824; Organist of St. Paul's Cathedral, London, 1838—1872; and Composer to the Chapel Royal, 1856—1872; received knighthood, 1872.

20, 118, 126, 166, 187, 210.

GOUNOD, CHARLES FRANCOIS. Born in Paris, 1818.

110.

HAUPTMANN, MORITZ, Doctor of Philosophy, Composer and eminent Theorist, and Cantor of the Thomas School at Leipzig. Born at Dresden, October 13, 1792. Died at Leipzig, January 3, 1868.

280.

HEAP, CHARLES SWINNERTON, Mus. D. Son of Robert James Heap. Born, April 10, 1847, at Birmingham.

In 1865 articled for two years to Dr. E. G. Monk, of York Minster; elected, in 1865, to the Mendelssohn Scholarship as Sullivan's successor; resided at Leipzig two and a-half years; resides now at Birmingham, following his profession. The Cambridge University conferred the degree of Mus. B. in 1870, and Mus. D. in 1871. He has been for ten years past the Conductor of the Birmingham Philharmonic Union.

270.

HIMMEL, FRIEDRICH HEINRICH. Born at Treuenbrietzen, Brandenburg, 1765. Died at Berlin, 1814.

Music Director to the King of Prussia.

285.

HOPKINS, EDWARD JOHN, Mus. D. Born in Westminster, 1818.

Chorister in the Chapel Royal, 1826—1833; Organist of Mitcham Church, Surrey, 1834; of St. Peter's, Islington, 1838; of St. Luke's, Berwick Street, London, 1841; of the Temple Church, London, 1843.

28, 121.

KENT, JAMES. Born at Winchester, 1700. Died there, 1776.

Chorister first in Winchester Cathedral, then in the Chapel Royal; Organist of Finedon, Northamptonshire; of Trinity College, Cambridge; of Winchester Cathedral and College, 1737—1774.

277.

MACFARREN, Sir GEORGE ALEXANDER, Mus. D., Cantab., 1875, Oxon., 1879. Son of Mr. George Macfarren. Born in London, 1818. Was knighted July 7, 1883.

Professor of Music in the University of Cambridge, 1875; Principal of the Royal Academy of Music, 1875.

292.

MENDELSSOHN-BARTHOLDY, FELIX JAKOB LUDWIG, Ph. D., Leipzig, 1836. Son of Abraham Mendelssohn. Born at Hamburg, 1809. Died at Leipzig, 1847.

312.

MOZART, JOHANNES CHRYSOSTOMUS WOLFGANG THEOPHILUS (GOTTLIEB or AMADEUS). Son of Leopold Mozart, Music Director to the Archbishop of Salzburg. Born at Salzburg, 1756. Died at Vienna, 1791.

107, 308.

NOVELLO, VINCENT. Son of Giuseppe Novello. Born in London, 1781. Died at Nice, 1861.

Chorister in the Sardinian Chapel, London; Organist of the Portuguese Chapel, London, 1797—1822; of the Roman Catholic Chapel, Moorfields, London, 1840—1843.

344.

OUSELEY, The Rev. Sir FREDERICK ARTHUR GORE, Bart., M.A., Oxon., 1849; Mus.D., Oxon., 1854; Mus. D., *ad eundem*, Durham, 1856; Mus. D., *ad eundem*, Cantab., 1862. Son of Sir William Gore Ouseley, Bart. Born in London, 1825.

Took Holy Orders, 1849; Professor of Music in the University of Oxford, 1855; Precenter of Hereford Cathedral, 1855; and Vicar of St. Michael's, Tenbury, 1856.

91, 274.

PURCELL, HENRY. Son of Henry Purcell, a Gentleman of the Chapel Royal. Born in London, 1658. Died there, 1695.

Chorister in the Chapel Royal, 1664; Organist of Westminster Abbey, 1680; Organist of the Chapel Royal, 1682.

114.

ROBERTS, JOHN VARLEY, Mus. D., Oxon. Son of Joseph Varley, born at Stanningley, near Leeds, Yorkshire, Sept. 25, 1841.

Was educated for the Cathedral Service; became Organist of St. John's Church, Farsley, near Leeds, at the age of 12; at 21 years of age, Organist of St. Bartholomew's Church, Armley, near Leeds; in 1868, after public competition, Organist and Choirmaster of the Parish Church, Halifax, Yorkshire, which position he still holds; in 1871 took Mus. Bac. degree at Oxford; in 1876 took Mus. D. degree at Oxford, and became a Fellow of the College of Organists, London.

His compositions are quite numerous, consisting of a sacred Cantata, "Jonah," Church Services, Anthems, Organ Voluntaries, Songs, etc., etc.

168.

SMITH, CHARLES W.

24.

SMITH, MONTEM. Son of Edward Woodley Smith, Lay-clerk of St. George's Chapel, Windsor.

Gentleman of the Chapel Royal; Vicar-choral of Westminster Abbey.

7.

STIRLING, ELIZABETH. Born at Greenwich, Kent, February 26, 1819.

Pupil of M. B. Wilson, Organist of St. Mary's, Greenwich, and Edward Holmes, Organist of All Saints, Poplar, London, where she was appointed Organist in 1839; also pupil for several years of Geo. A. Macfarren; in 1858 appointed Organist of St. Andrew's, Undershaft, London; resigned in 1880. In 1863 she married Mr. F. A. Bridge.

258.

www.ingramcontent.com/pod-product-compliance
Lightning Source LLC
Chambersburg PA
CBHW031128120726
47905CB00006B/1600